FORGET ME NEVER

GINA BLAXILL lives in London. She has an English degree from Cambridge University and now works in schools liaison, helping teenagers puzzle out the mysteries of higher education. Between the ages of eleven and fifteen she wrote an epic thirty-six-part story featuring over 1,000 characters – she still remembers most of their names!

Forget Me Never is Gina's second novel for young adults.

Also by Gina Blaxill

Pretty Twisted

FORGET ME NEVER

GINA BLAXILL

MACMILLAN

First published 2012 by Macmillan Children's Books
a division of Macmillan Publishers Limited
20 New Wharf Road, London N1 9RR
Basingstoke and Oxford
Associated companies throughout the world
www.panmacmillan.com

ISBN 978-1-4472-0806-8

A CIP catalogue record for this book is available from
the British Library.

Printed and bound by CPI Group (UK) Ltd, Croydon, CR0 4YY

To my brother Luke

SOPHIE

My cousin Danielle was twenty-six when she died. According to the police she jumped from the balcony of her flat, which, in the words of my foster-mother, wasn't a very nice way to go. What a stupid thing to say. Is death ever 'nice'?

My best friend Reece and I were the last people to see Dani alive. We'd been staying the weekend in her Bournemouth flat. I say her flat, but it actually belonged to Danielle's friend Fay, who was backpacking around South America and had said Dani was welcome to use it.

'Come over! It'll be brilliant.' Danielle had sounded so enthusiastic when she rang to invite me. 'Stay for a week, two weeks – I'm right next to the beach. Loads to do. You'll love it.'

'I've got school,' I said. 'They probably wouldn't approve of me taking a week out to splash about in the sea.'

'Oh, yeah, school. Bummer. Well, whatever. Let's make it a weekend.'

Timewise it wasn't ideal – it was just after Easter, and GCSE exams were breathing down my neck – but I went anyway. My foster-mum, Julie, was fine with me going – she said I deserved a break. I hadn't heard from Danielle in ages, even though until recently she'd been working in north London, where I was living.

So after school on Friday afternoon Reece and I got the train from Waterloo and Danielle met us on the platform at the other end, all smiles and carrying an enormous bag of rum-and-raisin fudge. She started chattering about the flat and the beach and her new job, which was a temporary one at an IT consultancy. We had fish and chips in town and then went for a walk along the seafront and tried out the fairground rides on the pier. Danielle knew the people running the air-rifle stand and they let us have a couple of free shots, which they probably regretted when Reece started arguing about the game's rules. Reece had always liked the sound of his own voice – Danielle and I found the whole thing terribly funny and couldn't stop laughing. It's not that remarkable, but I'll always hold on to that moment: a summer night when the light was starting to fade, a warm breeze ruffling my hair, sharing a joke with my cousin.

On Sunday afternoon Reece and I were getting ready to leave when the flat's doorbell buzzed. Danielle went to answer. I was in the other room at the time, so I don't know if she said anything to the caller over the intercom, but the next thing I knew, I could hear footsteps running downstairs.

'Does she always rush about like that?' Reece asked.

I shrugged. 'Pretty much.'

Reece went to the window, pressing his palms to it. 'She's talking to some bloke.'

'He's probably just selling something,' I said. 'Give me a hand with my case, will you? The zip's stuck.'

Half an hour later Danielle still hadn't come back. She wasn't outside the flat or picking up her mobile, so we had no choice but to head to the station. We'd booked two cheap seats on the 4.37 and I couldn't see Julie being happy about forking out for a later train.

'Bit off, Danielle not coming to say goodbye,' Reece said as we left. 'She's a bit of a skitz, your cousin.'

I felt a little disappointed that Danielle hadn't returned, but it wasn't as though it was the first time she'd let me down. She'd probably ring that evening, full of apologies.

Later Reece and I worked out that Danielle must have jumped from the balcony roughly around the time we were changing trains at Southampton. When I got back Julie told me what had happened.

I didn't believe it at first. The idea that Danielle could be gone seemed impossible. But when I began to take it all in – well, it was pretty tough. The next few days were terrible ones I'd give anything to forget. Over the years I'd become very good at blanking out feelings, but I couldn't ignore this. Dani had been the only person in the world who was mine, someone who knew exactly what I'd been through. She never judged me. She *understood*. That was something I could never replace.

The coroner was satisfied it was suicide. Danielle had never been that stable, I knew. She'd threatened to hurt herself before, and depression and mood swings ran in the family. Maybe it had been one of those freak decisions you'd never make if you could go back in time. In the words of the police officer who'd come to tell me the verdict, it was 'terribly sad, but it all made sense'.

The whole thing left me reeling, but very slowly I began to accept that there was nothing left for me to do but try to get on with my life – without Dani.

And maybe that's the way things would have gone if, four months later, I hadn't found the memory stick.

Summer. Weeks and weeks off school. Sunshine, Cornettos and flip-flops. Holidays abroad for the lucky ones. Muggy days that feel endless, hanging out with friends in the park. Fun. That's what summer should be, but this year it just wasn't working for me.

As well as coping with my grief I felt like I was at a crossroads, that everything was in flux. Everyone was waiting for their GCSE results. The exams had gone better than expected in the end, but I still couldn't see myself doing that well – English in particular had been a nightmare. Half of my year at Broom Hill High were leaving to go to colleges rather than staying on for the sixth form, which didn't have a great reputation. Lots of the teachers had gone on about how A levels and BTECs were a huge stepping stone and how the subjects we chose now could determine the rest of our lives. I wasn't sure I bought the idea that we were taking control; everyone still treated us like kids. Especially me – as a foster-kid I wasn't allowed to make my own decisions. I'd had to sit down with my social worker and come up with a 'Pathway Plan', supposedly to help me prepare for independent life when I turned eighteen and left care. Lorraine had strong opinions about what was best for me, and after a frustrated hour of trying to explain I had no idea where I wanted to be in two years, I gave up and let her take over. Biology, geography and law A levels would be as good as anything else.

Apart from helping out in the Save the Animals charity shop, something I'd been doing on-off ever since I'd come to live with Julie almost a year and a half ago, I had very little to do. I'd seen my old classmates down the high street. They'd invited me to join them, but after a couple of long afternoons sunbathing in the park I got restless. I'd rather be *doing* something. Hanging out is kind of empty when the people aren't really your friends; nothing gets said that you remember, and time seems to drag. It was easier for them if I wasn't around, anyway; putting up with someone who'd had a family member die was a real downer. It would have been easier if Dani had been knocked down by a car or had some kind of accident. That it had been suicide seemed to reflect on me somehow – especially as I had a reputation for being a bit crazy myself. The girls were clearly trying to treat me sensitively, but that just smacked home how different I was from them. It made me feel I would never be a normal teenager again.

I kept wondering how the summer break would have been different if Danielle was still here. Maybe we could have spent the summer in Bournemouth, just us – hanging out in town, clothes shopping, watching DVDs, the relaxed kind of stuff we didn't always fit into the weekends and evenings we spent together. Dani could be very inconsistent, sometimes going into moods that meant I wouldn't see her for weeks. But the absent patches had been worth it for the good ones, when she would be incredibly sweet, showering me with gifts and affection.

Instead I had my classmates and lots of school gossip I didn't want to hear. It just reminded me that I'd have to go back to Broom Hill, making me dread the end of the holidays even more than I was already. It was times like these that made me wish Reece hadn't left halfway through Year 10. Paloma, a girl who'd been in my class, had asked after him when I'd joined her gang in the park recently. Everyone still remembered Reece. His run-ins with teachers were legendary. One particular highlight was the time he calmly walked out of a history lesson and returned with an Internet printout that disproved what the teacher had just said about the causes of World War One. Reece had been excluded for that little stunt.

'So,' Paloma said, 'you still talk? You and Reece used to be totally buddy-buddy.'

'Yeah, well, that was before he buggered off to posh school,' I said. I knew I was being a little unfair – Reece had kicked up a huge fuss about being moved to Berkeley School for Boys, threatening his mother with a hunger strike and other ridiculous things. We'd stayed friends for a while, even arranging that Bournemouth trip so we could spend some proper time together. 'I'm fed up with him and his stupid new friends,' I added.

'Didn't seem like he'd changed last time I saw him, a couple of weeks before my party,' Paloma said. 'You were matey enough then.'

I started to make a daisy chain, not meeting her eyes. There was more to our falling-out, but I wasn't confiding in Paloma. I liked her best out of the girls from school because she stuck up for me – Paloma was sometimes teased about her weight, so she knew a thing or two about fighting back – but she did have a big mouth. Eventually she got the message and changed the subject, but I knew she'd try to get the full story later. When she invited me to the cinema the next day, I passed. Julie would have bugged me about that if she'd known. She was worried I didn't seem to have many friends. It wasn't true – there were always people for me to hang out with if I wanted – but I just wasn't close to anyone. Not like I had been to Dani, or to Reece.

I think maybe the reason I don't have many friends is that people are always so curious about my life. In the old days kids wanted to know what it was like to be in care, especially as I sometimes exaggerated the less pleasant bits. More recently I guess people just noticed me because I was different. Once I skived off school and went to Hampstead Heath instead, but I didn't get into trouble. Broom Hill's head teacher thought I was 'troubled', so he just sent me to have a long talk with the school counsellor. The other kids really resented that and said I'd got off easy. I used not to care about gossip, because people said stuff about Reece as well, but it's not so easy putting on a front on your own. Especially as since Paloma's party everyone really did have gossip about me. Horrible, embarrassing, true gossip.

Hendon, in north London, was where I lived. Reece used to say that if there was ever a nuclear war, the two things to survive would be Hendon and cockroaches, which tells you quite a bit about Hendon. I didn't think it was so bad – miles better than Hackney, where I used to live when I was being fostered by Mr and Mrs Ten Paces (whenever they went out she always walked about ten paces behind him. I didn't blame her – he was a bit weird, very picky about what she cooked for dinner, and he shouted at the telly a lot). Sure, Hendon had its share of fried-chicken shops and launderettes and depressing, poky newsagents, but there was Brent Cross shopping centre nearby, some quite decent parks and a big aeroplane museum.

My latest foster-mum, Julie, lived on an ordinary back road in a terraced house. It was OK – always noisy, as the two other foster-kids were primary-school age, but I could go out if it got too much. I'd miss it when it was time to move on. Julie had been very kind to me, especially since Dani died. When I'd mentioned I felt bad for not realizing how depressed Dani must have been, something Julie said had really stuck with me.

'You mustn't blame yourself for this, Sophie. Yes, you two were close – but people can be very good at hiding things. Danielle clearly didn't want you to know how sad she was feeling. It's hard to help someone who won't let you help them.'

Her words made me feel a little less guilty – though later I wondered if that last bit had been partly directed at me.

I was thinking about this the day I turned down Paloma's cinema offer. I'd decided to get busy to stop myself feeling bad about that, so I began to sew. Sewing, while an 'uncool' hobby, was something I really enjoyed. I liked to pick up clothes from the charity shop and customize them with unusual buttons and scraps of fabric.

I hadn't got anything particular I wanted to work on that

morning, so I dug through my wardrobe for inspiration. There were probably loads of old clothes I'd forgotten about at the back. Sure enough, I found some – including stuff that had belonged to Danielle.

'Jesus Christ,' I muttered. Lots of her things had been passed on to me, but that didn't stop me feeling odd about it, now that she'd gone. I pulled out a pair of Dani's jeans and held them against me. They'd be a good fit. Maybe I could lop a couple of inches off the legs and wear them as cut-offs.

There was a funny bulge in the pocket of the jeans. It was a memory stick. I knew it wasn't mine – I always used the ones school issued us with. It had to be Danielle's.

May as well have a look, I thought, booting up Edith, my laptop. She had been Dani's, and Dani had lent her to me that last weekend to help me with my GCSE revision. I'd called her Edith because she was a bit slow and unsteady, like a little old lady. When Edith finally allowed me to view the USB's contents, I saw folders of photos pop up. Curious, I clicked on the first and saw a familiar face.

I swear the world stopped moving. It was Danielle, posing with a brightly coloured cocktail. I'd never seen this photo before. I only had a few ancient pictures of her. I opened up more folders – these were Danielle too. God, I must have stumbled upon her entire photo collection.

Almost heady with excitement, I scrolled through, eager

to view each new snapshot into my cousin's life. After a couple of albums though, I had to pause.

It was too much, too much all at once. I felt a little floaty, as though part of me was somewhere else. They captured parts of her life I'd never known existed, and they made me realize how many opportunities I'd missed to get to know her better. And now, I never would.

It felt like someone had punched me hard in the gut, slamming home the emotions I was usually so good at ignoring. Tears spilt down my cheeks, my heart pounding.

I don't know how long I sat there. Eventually my tears dried and I curled up on my bed, feeling exhausted. I looked across at the picture that was still on the screen. It was from a folder labelled 'Party'. It showed Danielle standing in a door frame, wearing a floral smock over skinny jeans and at least three different necklaces.

I look a lot like her now, I thought. We both took after our mums, who'd been sisters. The same fair complexion, long necks, strong eyebrows and dark hair, though Dani's had always been dead straight while mine had a wave to it. We had different builds – Dani was curvier and shorter than I was. Apparently height was something I'd got from my dad – not that I would know. I'd never met him, and what I knew about him barely covered a Post-it note. He probably didn't know I existed.

After a while I got up and returned to my desk. I didn't

really want to look at the photos any more, but I also didn't feel like I could do anything else. As I browsed further, I began to realize that Danielle had had a boyfriend. He was in a lot of the party shots and it looked like they'd gone on holiday together too. I half smiled; Danielle had always been obsessed with the sun, even though we both burned rather than tanned. The boyfriend was cute too, if you liked that kind of thing – he looked a bit like he'd stepped out of a boy band, with carefully ruffled blond hair and a photogenic smile, and he seemed to like wearing tight T-shirts that showed off his six-pack. The photos showed the date in the bottom left-hand corner – three months before Danielle had died.

I wondered where he was now and why Dani had never mentioned him to me. He definitely hadn't been at her funeral – they must have split up. Maybe she'd been really gutted. That could even have been the reason she'd killed herself, and why she'd hidden her depression from me. Though I'd never have said it, I'd always thought Dani was needy around people. She was incredibly quick to trust, something I noticed because I was the opposite, and I suspected part of her generosity sprang from wanting to be liked. It seemed a bit of a contradiction for someone academically smart like Dani to be so naive, but I guess book-smarts don't necessarily equal being streetwise.

The clock in the hall chimed; I jumped. Twelve o'clock – I'd been looking at photos for well over an hour. Realizing how dry my throat was, I went downstairs and picked up a can of cola. Luckily Julie and the kids were out – I didn't fancy explaining why my face was so red and blotchy.

Is it good or bad that I found the memory stick? I asked myself as I returned to my room. Bad – because I felt awful, and somehow I knew this sense of loss wasn't going to ever leave me. But good too – because now I had more to remember my cousin by.

I looked through the photos again, pausing on a shot of Danielle's boyfriend. I hadn't paid it much attention the first time – it was poorly composed, perhaps taken by accident – but this time something about it made me look more closely.

I frowned, chewing the top of my straw and blowing bubbles into my cola. He reminded me of someone . . .

I still hadn't figured it out an hour later when I grabbed lunch – a banana sandwich and a handful of raisins. It was only after I'd finished altering the jeans that I remembered.

The day before Danielle had died we'd been in town, which was teeming with Saturday crowds. It wasn't the easiest shopping expedition – Dani and I wanted to do the clothes shops, but Reece had made loud noises about being bored, and when I'd poked my head into a New Age place that looked interesting, Dani had said it was a load of rubbish that only nutters believed in. To keep the peace we'd stuck to department stores and gadget and music shops. We were just coming out of HMV when Danielle froze. There was a man further down the street, waving at her.

'Dani?' I'd asked. 'You OK?'

Danielle grabbed my arm. 'I'm sick of town. Let's get back to the flat.'

Reece and I exchanged a look but did as she said. A bus was passing and we jumped on. Danielle pressed her nose to the window, looking back towards the street we'd come from. She seemed to relax once the bus turned the corner. When I asked her about the man, she laughed.

'Oh, that's just someone from work. Super-annoying – drones on for hours about the most boring things. We've had a lucky escape!'

Reece and I had accepted this explanation and forgotten about it. But now I knew otherwise – because the man waving at Dani had been the boyfriend in the photo. Or at least . . . I was fairly certain it was. But had his hair been blond? I remembered it being darker . . .

Suddenly I wasn't sure. My memory of him was like one of those painting-by-numbers pictures you get given as a kid – outline sketched out, but minus any details until you add the colour.

Maybe it didn't really matter. Danielle was dead.

Whether or not the man in the Bournemouth street was the boyfriend didn't change that. But heck, I still wanted to *know*.

If only I could get a second opinion . . .

REECE

The last thing I'd been expecting to find in my inbox when I logged in that Wednesday morning was an email from Sophie Hayward, my ex-best friend. But there it was – untitled and out of the blue.

> Hi Reece,
> If you haven't instantly deleted this, I need to talk to you. It's about Danielle. It won't take long. Can we meet up? Text me. My number's still the same.
> Ta.
> Soph

I read it again, frowning. The bowl of porridge I'd been eating sat in front of me going cold. What an odd coincidence. I'd been thinking about Soph quite a bit this summer, even though we hadn't talked for months – probably because I'd been spending a fair bit of time on Sticky Wicket, an online cricket forum for teenagers. Like most forums, many of the members were idiots, but they were always fun to pick arguments with.

Back when we were mates, I'd even argued with Sophie on the forum. Soph was the only girl I'd ever met who actually understood the rules of cricket. That was one of the reasons we'd first made friends. I later found out that her initial motivation for getting into cricket was that her mum had once hinted her dad liked it.

It was three months ago that Sophie ditched me, back at the start of May. I was still unclear as to why, and I doubted I'd find out. Nothing was ever simple with Sophie. I used to joke that she thought so much that I was surprised her brain didn't explode.

As far as our friendship went, the end had come shortly after my stupid school play. I'd been forced into it by the drama teacher. He said it'd be a 'good use for my big mouth'.

The play was *Measure for Measure*, which was, predictably, Shakespeare. Mum got irritatingly involved. She wrote my lines down on Post-it notes and stuck them all over the house – on my wardrobe, the fridge, even by the loo roll, something my little sister Neve found hilarious. 'It's so you can't help but learn them,' Mum explained. 'This is incredibly important to your future, darling – Berkeley's produced some really well-known actors. It's a great honour to be in one of their plays.'

Quite who these actors were I didn't know, and neither, I suspected, did she.

'But I don't want to be an actor,' I pointed out. 'Anyway, I know my lines. I told Sophie I'd be online now.'

'Practice makes perfect, Reece,' Mum said primly. 'I'm sure Sophie wouldn't mind your not talking to her tonight. It's not like she's your girlfriend.'

I decided to ignore that last bit. Mum wouldn't understand that I used to see Sophie every day at school and never ran out of things to say. I was trying hard to keep up with her properly. It wasn't easy, not being at the same school any more, especially now I had new mates who wanted to see me too. Soph didn't seem keen on them for some reason.

By the time the day of the performance came, I was kinda looking forward to it. Sophie was coming. We hadn't seen much of each other that week and there wouldn't be much of a chance to catch up the night of the play. But there'd be time for that at Paloma Watson's party, which was on Saturday.

The show went smoothly. As soon as I'd changed out of my costume I made a getaway and met Sophie and Mum in the foyer. Mum had wanted to bring Neve too, but I'd managed to talk her into getting Aunt Meg to babysit. I didn't think two hours of Jacobean verse was the kind of thing even the most cultured three-year-old would get a kick out of.

'Well done, darling!' Before I could stop her, Mum grabbed me and planted a kiss on my forehead. 'I heard the parents sitting behind me whispering about how good you were. I wanted to turn around and say, "That's *my* son!" but I didn't want to interrupt your big moment—'

'Mum! Stop it,' I begged. Embarrassing or what! I looked at Sophie. She had her hands shoved into her pockets and wasn't meeting my eyes.

'What's up?' I whispered as we walked out. 'The play wasn't *that* bad, surely.'

'It was fine,' Sophie muttered. 'I'd better go now.'

'It's only nine. Come over for an hour. Some of my mates are coming. Unofficial after-show party.'

Sophie made a face and instantly I felt annoyed. She never made any effort with my Berkeley mates. They thought she was bad-tempered and moody. I wasn't sure they believed me when I explained she was a different person when we were alone.

'See you at Paloma's at the weekend then,' I said.

Sophie shrugged. 'Parties aren't really my thing. Always feel out of place.'

'You might feel more comfortable if you looked the part more,' I said. 'I mean, you look cool whatever you wear, but if you dressed up a bit sometimes, it might make you fit in better.'

I nodded at two girls my mates were talking to. They were both wearing sleeveless tops and short skirts, maybe a bit overdressed, but it got my point across. Sophie stared at them, then mumbled that she was going home. I began wondering if she was interested in staying friends with me at all. It felt like I bent over backwards to meet up with her, and nine times out of ten I was the one to text or email. From the way she behaved sometimes, maybe I shouldn't have bothered.

'She's probably just moving on,' Mum said the next afternoon. Neve was nearby watching *Postman Pat*, nose almost touching the screen. 'Sad, but it happens. Why don't you invite some friends from school over next week to take your mind off her?'

'Things were just dandy until recently,' I said. 'I sent her a text today. She never even replied! What's changed?'

'Be fair, Reece,' Mum said. 'Don't forget, it's only been a few months since that dreadful business with her cousin. Bereavement can affect people in strange ways – as you well know.'

Mum actually sticking up for Soph shocked me into silence. She was right. Danielle's death had unsettled me enough. We'd been eating lunch with her like everything was normal, then a few hours later she was gone. Totally surreal. And how I felt must be nothing next to what Sophie must be feeling.

Maybe I hadn't been looking out for her enough. But beyond being there for her and keeping in touch, I wasn't sure how I could help. I didn't think Sophie would ever really open up to me about Danielle.

'Anyway,' Mum continued, 'Sophie's a young woman now. She probably wants to hang out with girlfriends and talk girl stuff. It's quite unusual for a girl and boy to have a friendship like yours at this age.'

'Mum, you know that's stereotypical bullshit.'

'Less of the language!' Mum snapped, quickly looking at Neve to see if she was listening. She wasn't. 'Picked up at Broom Hill, no doubt; it's a good job you're out of that place. I never liked your having to mix with those kids from the Raspberry Valley Estate.'

I rolled my eyes. 'You didn't mind me going there before we got Dad's life-insurance money.'

'Oh, don't go on, Reece! I was only trying to be helpful.' She smiled, patting the sofa seat next to her. 'Why don't we watch a film together once Neve's in bed? I could make some popcorn.'

As I yawned my way through *Pride and Prejudice* with my mother, I hoped Sophie was OK. She could do funny things when she was in a mood. I sent her an email, and several more texts over the next few days. She didn't reply. So eventually I decided to leave it. That Saturday I went out with my Berkeley mates rather than to Paloma's party. When the next week went by without any contact from Sophie, I got the message. So I did something I never do and gave up.

And now, months later, Sophie had emailed me. I didn't need to mull things over. I knew what my response was going to be.

Long time no speak, I typed. **How's this afternoon?**

SOPHIE

By the time I got off the bus at Muswell Hill, it was a quarter past five. The Broadway was just as I remembered – but then, why would it have changed? It hadn't been *that* long since I'd last been to Reece's. It was one of the nicest days of summer so far – warm but not sweltering – and I was enjoying the feeling of the sun on my legs. I was wearing denim shorts, a long-sleeved polka-dot top I'd made from what had once been an oversize dress, and a sunhat with a wide brim – all charity-shop stuff.

Reece's house was about ten minutes from the Broadway, but he'd asked me to meet him at the school cricket pitch. The club he played for was an independent one but they used Berkeley's facilities for their practice sessions. This didn't fit in with my plans of showing him Dani's photos, but it was easier to come to his neck of the woods – I could always leave if things got too awkward.

I'd been to Reece's school several times before. It's one of those old red-brick buildings with fancy doorway arches and stained-glass windows, and there are statues of former headmasters dotted about the grounds that stare at you disapprovingly. Berkeley is way up the education league tables; you can only go there if you're loaded.

I started dragging my feet as I got closer. I felt mixed-up – nervous, hesitant and slightly resentful. I never liked going near Berkeley – it reminded me of just how little I had. And what would it be like seeing Reece again after all this time? Everything to do with him – the memories, the in-jokes – I'd closed myself off from them, put them into a little mental box with a sticker that said 'over' on it. I wasn't sure how it would feel to open that box again. Everything that had happened still hurt. I knew Reece probably didn't see it that way – but he didn't know the full story.

I saw Reece before he saw me. All the boys on the field were wearing cricket whites and for a moment I wasn't sure which one he was. It looked like practice had just broken up – half the players were hanging around chatting while the others were clearing up. I stood a little way back, hoping they wouldn't notice. I knew Reece's friends looked down on me. But one of them spotted me and said something, sniggering. Reece gave him a withering look and came over, tucking his bat under his arm. For an awkward moment we sort of hovered in front of each other, not quite sure whether there was going to be a hug or not.

'So . . .' Reece let the word hang in the air a moment and it became obvious there wasn't. 'That was a very random email this morning. What gives?'

He looked quite different from how he had three months ago, mainly because he was wearing his hair in a side parting. It made him look a lot older; I wasn't sure I liked that – and I definitely didn't like that his voice had picked up a hint of the clear-cut, posh way his friends spoke. The other change was that he'd grown. One of Reece's big gripes had always been that I was taller than him – but then I was taller than most people in our year, including the boys. I still had a good inch on him though.

'I wanted to speak to you,' I said.

'Evidently. Must be something fairly seismic. You made it pretty clear after the play you didn't want anything to do with me.'

Reece's friends passed us, grinning. One of them wolf-whistled.

'Shut up, you ignorant tossers!' Reece called after them.

'Like I said in the email, it's about Danielle,' I said, ignoring Reece's jibe about us not speaking, and I started explaining what was on the memory stick. Reece arched his eyebrows and I realized how wishy-washy it all sounded. It probably looked like I was making a lame excuse to see him again.

'I see,' Reece said. 'In that case, you'd better come back to mine, hadn't you?'

Reece's road was, by anyone's standards, a lovely place to live, with big, detached and very expensive new-build houses, just a short walk from Berkeley. I was sure that Reece's mum Effie, arch-snob, had chosen it for that reason. She sang the school's praises so regularly that I was surprised they hadn't asked her to write their prospectus.

Reece unlocked the door. The hallway smelt of air freshener and there was a wooden rack for those entering to place their shoes. The walls were lined with precisely arranged photographs in identical frames. At the end was a big picture of Colin, Reece's dad. I'd always liked that one because, unlike the others, mostly school photos of Reece, it looked natural, with Colin glancing over his shoulder, half amused, half surprised. He had been a nice guy, Colin.

'I'm going to have a shower,' Reece announced, dumping his sports kit at the bottom of the stairs. 'Get yourself a drink and then we'll check out the memory stick.'

'Reece?' It was Effie. It sounded as if her voice was coming from the sitting room. 'Who are you talking to?'

'Mum? Weren't you supposed to be out?'

'I was waiting for you. Meg says she's not well and can't take Neve, so I was hoping you'd stay in with her, else I'll have to miss my class. Did you leave your phone at home again?' Effie bustled into the hallway. Her face froze when she saw me and I gave a nervous laugh.

'Sophie,' Effie said, her expression fixing into a polite smile. 'What a surprise. Haven't seen you for a while.'

'Be back down in ten,' Reece said, and headed up the stairs. Oh, great – cheers, Reece, I thought murderously.

'Put those sweaty cricket clothes in the linen basket this time, not on the floor!' Effie turned to me. I had to give it to her – Effie was looking good. She'd had a rich auburn colour put on her hair, and while the T-shirt and denim skirt she wore were casual, they were well cut and obviously expensive. I suppose if I had money to splash about like she did, I might give myself a makeover too.

'Would you like a drink?' Effie asked, heading to the kitchen. 'We have juice or lemonade, or I'm sure Reece wouldn't mind you having one of his disgusting energy drinks.'

'Lemonade's fine.' I followed her through. A small girl was sitting at the breakfast bar, busily scribbling away on coloured sugar paper. She looked up when I entered.

'Neve, do you remember Sophie?' Effie said, going to the cupboard and taking out a glass. 'Reece's friend.'

Neve gave me a sly look and put the end of a crayon in her mouth. 'Secret,' she said.

'What are you talking about?' Effie asked, but Neve said she wasn't telling. I slid on to one of the seats. Neve must have had her third birthday by now – I remembered when she was a tiny ugly-looking thing with squinty eyes, that just cried a lot. She looked quite a lot like Reece now, I thought.

'Where did you go?' Neve asked as I accepted the drink Effie poured for me.

'Nowhere special. Just getting on with things.' I hoped Reece wasn't going to take a long shower.

'What things?'

'Things things,' I said.

'Things things things!' Neve laughed. 'I'm going to draw you!'

She got out a fresh piece of paper and grabbed the purple crayon, even though I wasn't wearing anything that colour. Glad that Neve wasn't going to press the issue of where exactly I'd been, I looked at Effie. She was watching me, lips pursed.

'So, er, how are you?' I asked. I had to say something – the heavy silence was making my skin prickle.

'Very well, thank you for asking,' Effie said rather primly. 'And how are you?'

'OK.'

'Are you enjoying life with your new family?'

She made it sound as though I'd purchased Julie in a shop.

'They're not exactly new,' I said. 'I've been there a year and a half now. But yeah, it's fine.'

'How do foster-homes work exactly? Do they have you until you turn eighteen and then they leave you to get on with things?'

What a way with words she had. I avoided the temptation to answer sarcastically and explained about my Pathway Plan, though I didn't go into details. I knew Effie was only asking so she could turn her nose up. She'd never liked me.

According to her, I had 'problems' and 'a bad background'. I'd heard her and Colin talking about it one night when I was about twelve – they hadn't known Reece and I were in the next room.

Effie switched the conversation to my studies and I filled her in on my A-level choices. We were searching for something else to say when Neve interrupted by waving her masterpiece in my face. The sugar paper showed a stick woman wearing a massive pair of shorts, with dark hair that fell to the ground and some sort of mask on her face.

'That's great, Neve! Am I a superhero or a burglar?' I asked.

'Burglar.'

'Ah right, what did I steal?'

'Cakes,' Neve said. 'Cream ones.'

Reece appeared in T-shirt and jeans, rubbing his hair with a towel.

'Right, let's go up,' he said, grabbing a bottle of Lucozade from the fridge and dumping the towel on the counter. 'See you later, Mum.'

'Wait a minute,' Effie said. 'I'm off in an hour. Are you going to stay in for Neve?'

Reece sighed and huffed, which Effie seemed to take as acceptance. 'If you and Sophie want dinner later, I'll leave some cash out. There are takeaway menus in the drawer.'

I followed Reece up to his room. Like the rest of the

house, it was neat and tidy, though this was probably down to the cleaner. Books, mainly textbooks and sports autobiographies, were neatly lined up on the shelves. The top one was reserved for the collection of old *Beano* and *Dandy* annuals that had belonged to Reece's dad.

Reece flipped on the flash new computer that sat on the desk. It had been his birthday a few weeks ago – I guessed the computer had been a present. He pulled up a stool next to his swivel chair.

'Let's have a look at this USB then. Better do it pronto, before Mum offs and leaves me babysitting the poddling.'

'Look, Reece . . . you don't have to be so *businesslike* about all this. I know you're pissed off with me, but this passive-aggressive stuff is a pain.' As soon as the words came out I regretted them.

Reece scowled. 'Why shouldn't I be passive-aggressive and businesslike? You're the one who ditched me for no reason.'

'Not for no reason. You let me down.'

'How? I made time for you when I moved schools. I was there!'

'Not the night of Paloma's party, you weren't. You were out with your new friends, having a whale of a time, judging by the Facebook photos.'

'What's the big deal? Did something happen at the party? You told me at the play that you weren't even going.'

'Look, I didn't come to talk about that! Stop going on.'

Reece muttered something, then to my surprise shut up. I handed him the USB. A little gruffly I said, 'Look in the party folder, ninth photo.'

He opened it up. I watched him frown at the screen. He paused, then flicked through a few more pictures. Impatient, I said, 'Come on, you must know. Is it him, d'you reckon?'

'Oh, he's the dude from town all right. But . . .' Reece hesitated. 'I'm pretty certain – ninety per cent sure – that this is the same bloke that came by the flat too. The one who rang the bell for Danielle when we were getting ready to leave.'

'What? How can you tell?'

'Got a look at him out of the window, didn't I? OK, so we were four floors up and it was a few months ago, but I'd swear to it. Didn't connect them at the time. So what's the deal with this, Soph? D'you think he had something to do with – you know . . . ?'

I hesitated. It was a good question – and I was almost afraid of answering it.

Slowly I said, 'Maybe . . . I mean, think about it. There was the scene in town, when she was upset to see him. Then the next day she went off with him when he called at the flat. A couple of hours later she jumps off that balcony. That's no coincidence, right? And it's not the only thing that bugs me. Remember what the eyewitness said in the inquest report? That old lady? She saw Dani fall – back first. Why backwards?' I paused. 'And . . . aside from that, I've been thinking. I'm not convinced that Dani *was* depressed enough to take her own life. I accepted it to begin with, but don't you remember what she was like that weekend? She was talking about the things she wanted to buy when she got paid, about the future. Would someone suicidal do that? I'm not saying anything sinister went on – but I'm just not convinced it's so simple. Dani seemed fine.'

'Might have *seemed* fine. Doesn't mean she was. Anyway, aren't you implying that this guy gave her a reason to do it?'

'Maybe – I don't know.' Suddenly embarrassed, I looked away. Ridiculous – coming here with crazy theories when I hadn't spoken to Reece in months. I needed to find someone else to dump on – I probably sounded a bit hysterical.

'I'll go,' I said, getting to my feet. 'Thanks for helping.'

I was almost at the door when Reece said, 'Sure you've been OK?'

His voice almost sounded soft. I looked over my shoulder.

'I'm fine. What d'you mean?'

'You know. Just generally.'

Was he saying that he'd been worried about me when we weren't speaking?

'I really am fine,' I said firmly. 'And I really am going.'

'You know what I think,' Reece said. 'There's no way

your cousin seeing that guy was prearranged. She was definitely shocked to see him in town. Whatever he needed to say to her at the flat, it must have been significant.'

He was juggling an eraser from hand to hand, and now he added a key ring and the memory stick.

'Don't throw that about,' I said, marching over and snatching it, annoyed that I'd almost forgotten it. 'It's valuable.'

Reece threw the eraser against the wall. It made a pinging sound and bounced underneath the bed.

'How long had Dani been living in Bournemouth?'

'Dunno. A couple of weeks.'

'Where was she before?'

'Somewhere in Archway. What are you thinking?'

'Well, let's assume the bloke doesn't live in Bournemouth. That they met in London and he made a special trip to see her. You don't usually do that when people aren't expecting you, especially as Bournemouth's hardly just down the road.'

Despite myself I was impressed with his reasoning. 'Must have been something he couldn't email or call her about.'

'Doesn't mean it was anything suspicious though. We know he was gone by the time Dani fell. The eyewitness said there was no one else on the balcony.'

'I'm not saying he *pushed* her,' I said, aware that I was starting to sound silly again. 'I'm just saying that we now know this guy is Dani's ex, and him visiting might be significant in some way.'

Reece turned to the computer and opened Firefox. He went on to Facebook and opened the In Memoriam page that one of Danielle's friends had created. Lots of people, including me and Reece, had left messages. It had seemed the right thing to do. Julie said it trivialized her death, but in my opinion it was the best way for all the people who knew her to come together. The page showed a posed profile picture of Dani at a friend's wedding, confetti in her hair and toasting the camera with a wine glass.

Reece was scrolling down the comments. Beginning to realize what he was doing, I sat back on the stool.

'Stop,' I said. 'That's him, there. Aiden Anderson.'

Aiden Anderson hadn't written much in his message – just **RIP babe, you'll be missed x**. Reece clicked and his profile page popped up, a big photo of him on the left.

'How's that for awesome detective work?' Reece said, looking smug. 'Sherlock would be proud.'

There wasn't much on Aiden's page – he seemed to be an advocate of the 'I'm so cool I keep my profile practically empty' school of social networking.

'What now?' Reece said. 'Do we sit on this information, or do something with it?'

'You mean, go to the police? What do *you* think?'

He shrugged. 'Your cousin. You decide.'

I picked at the threads on the bottom of my shorts. It felt very surreal to be sitting here on a nice summer evening, talking about Dani's death. I'd thought about it constantly, but until now I'd never questioned the verdict. Part of me wished I hadn't started this. I wondered if Reece was taking it seriously. He was being so matter-of-fact that I suspected he wasn't. Maybe he thought that I couldn't deal with Dani killing herself and just wanted someone to blame. And maybe I did. I didn't know what I thought any more – just that I needed to do something.

'If I go to the police, will you come with me?' I asked.

Reece got up. 'I suddenly hear chow mein calling. Want to order takeaway?'

'Answer my question. I'm serious.'

'I'm considering it,' Reece said. 'But my brain needs MSG first.'

Rolling my eyes, I followed him downstairs. Effie was by the door, about to head out. After laying down a few house rules, which Reece no doubt already knew and were probably said for my benefit, she disappeared, leaving us with Neve.

Reece picked up the phone and ordered some chow mein, seaweed, sweet and sour pork, black bean beef and prawn crackers.

'Yum,' he said. 'They give massive portions, this place. We'll be stuffed.'

'Like turkeys,' said Neve happily.

'Hooray,' I said.

Catching me looking at him, Reece said, 'Look, I'll come with you – purely because it'll be more interesting than what I was planning on doing. Happy?'

I supposed it was too much to hope that he'd agree with me. It was funny – since we'd started talking, the posh note in his voice had gone. He sounded more like the old Reece. Well, better him on my side than no one. I was normally good at doing difficult things by myself, but this was something I'd rather not face alone.

REECE

Sophie left straight after we'd eaten. As soon as I was sure she was well gone I grabbed a cushion and gave it a good pummelling. When I'd let off enough steam I threw it on the carpet and switched the telly on to an angry rock radio station. Neve shrank back, looking worried. Quickly I turned the volume down.

'I'm not mad at you, sweetie,' I said. 'It's just teenager stuff. You wouldn't understand.'

Sophie was messing me about and I didn't like it. She'd waltzed back into my life, assuming my help was hers for the taking. The stubborn part of me had wanted to say no – smack rejection in her face and see how she liked it. But I couldn't help hoping the Danielle stuff was just an excuse for getting in contact.

I was half annoyed I hadn't given her a rougher time. I'd just been nice and helpful, two things I'm usually very definitely not. Perhaps it was unfair, but it felt like I'd been taken advantage of. I got how horrible it was for Sophie to lose Danielle, and what a struggle dealing with grief was – I'd gone through it with my dad. I also got how rubbish it was to be left questioning whether the death was as clear cut as everyone said. It just would have made all the difference to hear an apology for the months she'd ignored me.

Naff all was going to happen with the police tomorrow.

Shooting theories was one thing, and Soph was right in saying there were things that didn't add up, but it was way too fanciful to seriously believe Aiden Anderson turning up had anything to do with Danielle jumping off that balcony. That would make it *murder* – a huge accusation. While I'd never say so to Sophie, I'd always thought Danielle was a bit of a fruitcake – shoving ice cream and sweets in our faces like we were Neve's age. Acting like she adored Sophie one minute, then vanishing for months on end the next. But despite everything I had liked her, though I couldn't say I really got her, not like Sophie did.

I was far more curious about what would happen when we were done with the police. Would Sophie walk away from me again? Or would she want to make up? And where might that lead?

SOPHIE

I spent most of the next morning in Save the Animals sorting through bags of donations, picking out the items we could sell. Doing something brainless is the best therapy sometimes.

At two o'clock I met Reece outside Hendon Central station. He was holding a white paper bag and a bottle of lemon Lucozade.

'Went to one of the Jewish bakeries,' he said, mouth full. It was hard to make out what he was saying over the roar of the traffic. 'Want a spinach boreka?'

'Spinach? Gross! Why d'you always choose the disgusting flavours? The sweet ones are much nicer.'

'Cos I don't want you scoffing my lunch, that's why. Hendon hasn't changed much, has it? Same old dump.' He swallowed. 'OK, my stomach's happy now. Let's do this.'

It was cool inside the police station, a welcome change from the baking heat. The foyer needed renovating; the plastic chairs in the waiting room looked like they belonged in a school, and the walls were a mucky cream colour I guessed had once been white. No wonder they were plastered with posters.

The officer at the front desk gave us a sceptical look –

probably already thinking we were time-wasters. 'Can I help?'

'Yeah,' I said, wetting my lips. 'Four months ago there was a suicide your Bournemouth colleagues investigated. I've got new information.'

'So've I,' Reece said, not to be outdone.

'One at a time,' the woman said. 'I'll get someone to speak to you.'

Another officer appeared. She took us to a side room and asked us to explain. 'I'll need to take your details,' she said. 'Do you have the case reference number – or precise dates?'

'You know they only want your details so they can use them later,' Reece whispered. 'Wake up tomorrow and I guarantee your inbox will be full of spam warnings about drugs and unlicensed minicabs. It's direct marketing. They did a feature about it on *Watchdog*. Once you're on a list there's no escape.'

'The police are the ones protecting us from that kind of thing, idiot.' I elbowed him in the ribs and gave the officer the information she'd asked for. She took everything down, then told us someone would be in touch to ask us to come for an interview in the company of an appropriate adult. We found ourselves politely but firmly escorted to the door, a wave of heat and sunlight hitting us as we stepped out.

'Waste of time,' Reece said. 'Suppose we should have anticipated that.'

I nodded, trying not to show my apprehension. Somehow I couldn't see Julie being thrilled about this. Why was nothing ever simple?

The police rang later that day and asked me to come in the next morning. Julie, who'd taken the call, shook her head as she put the receiver back into its cradle.

'All right, Sophie. What's this *really* about?'

'There isn't any "really".' I felt irked by the hint of accusation in her voice. 'I didn't realize you'd need to get involved.'

Julie didn't look convinced, but the following morning we went to the police station. There was a different officer on reception this time and we were told to wait for a Detective Inspector Perry. Ten minutes later a man walked in. He was probably around fifty, with a thick beard and moustache that were going grey. He looked a bit like Father Christmas.

'Sophie Hayward? And you must be Sophie's foster-mother. I'm DI Perry.'

'Julie Coombes.' Julie shook his hand.

Perry took us into a small, brightly lit room with a rectangular table and more plastic chairs. Another man, whom Perry introduced as Detective Constable Grace, was setting up a tape recorder. He was quite young and a bit spotty. I wondered if this was one of his first cases.

'So . . .' Perry said, leaning back in his chair. I decided I liked his manner; it was relaxed, leisurely even. 'I've looked at the notes the sergeant took yesterday and had a word with my colleagues in Bournemouth. I understand you came across some photographs of your cousin.'

I was distracted from replying by a noise from down the corridor; it sounded like someone yelling. I wondered if Reece was being interviewed today too.

I told them about the USB. Out of the corner of my eye I caught Julie giving me a hard look and realized how sketchily I'd explained this to her. I'd be in for it later. I handed the USB to Perry when he asked for it and was given a receipt. I'd copied the photos on to Edith before coming out.

'This might not seem like a big deal, but I really don't think she jumped because she was depressed,' I said. I described all the plans Danielle had been making. 'She had . . . issues, but she was doing OK. Reece will back me up.'

'We've seen Danielle's medical records,' said Perry. 'She had a history of depression. The conclusion my Bournemouth colleagues came to was that this was almost certainly a contributory factor for her death – especially as the post-mortem showed she hadn't been taking her medication. How did she seem to you that weekend?'

I was going to answer, 'Normal,' but changed my mind –

Dani didn't really have a 'normal' mode in the way most people did. 'OK, I guess.'

'How close were you to your cousin?' Perry asked. 'Talk me through your relationship.'

I hesitated. Perry seemed kind, but he was still a stranger and this was personal.

'I didn't know her well when I was little,' I said. 'She was eleven years older than me, and I went into care when I was seven. We got close after . . . well, our mums died together.'

It had been a car accident five years ago. It wasn't clear where they'd been heading, but it was clear that both of them were well over the limit. They'd swerved off the road at a junction – thankfully no other cars were involved. Even though I'd not lived with Mum for several years and rarely saw her, it still made a huge impact. The best way to describe how I felt was numb. At least Dani had been going through the same thing. That shared experience gave us a bond nothing could break. Her being around made me feel better. Not only about Mum, but about a lot of things. We just 'got' each other.

Perry nodded, looking sympathetic. Slightly reassured, I said, 'Dani had got her life together. She'd finished a course in computing and got a decent job. She was proud of that – sometimes she was scatty, but never at work. Computers made more sense to her than people did, I think.'

'Did you see much of her once she started work?' Perry asked.

'Sometimes when she was down I didn't see her for a while,' I admitted. 'We only met when she was happy — which is why her killing herself that weekend just doesn't make sense.'

Perry asked about the photos and how I'd made the link to Aiden Anderson. Now that I was explaining, in this bright, serious little room, it sounded a bit daft, like something a teenager might do because she was bored and wanted attention. I could tell Julie wasn't buying it; she wasn't saying anything, but she's not difficult to read.

'I'm not messing about, or saying that he pushed her,' I said when I'd finished explaining. 'Not exactly. I'm just sure it's worth investigating.'

'Do you think whatever passed between Danielle and the man you're calling Aiden Anderson could have left her worked up enough to take her own life? I mean, rather than her mental state?' Grace said suddenly. I'd almost forgotten he was there; evidently he'd been listening after all.

'I don't know,' I said. 'From what Reece says, she seemed agitated when she saw him outside the flat, and she definitely was when she saw him in town.'

Perry stood, nodding for Grace to turn off the recording. 'Thanks for coming to see us, Sophie — you've done the right thing. We'll speak to your friend Reece and see if we can have a word with Mr Anderson. We'll be in touch.'

'OK,' I said. I must have sounded unconvinced, because Perry said, 'Don't worry, Sophie. If there's anything untoward, we'll find it.'

Julie and I walked home in silence. As we let ourselves into the house, I said, 'You're not happy.'

'Can't say I am,' Julie said with a sigh.

'It's not like I wanted to drag you down there,' I said stiffly. 'Didn't mean to cause you any trouble.'

'It's OK. Stuff happens, Sophie. If this means an extra social-worker visit, so be it – it'll be nice to have some adult company.' She flashed me a smile. The adult-company comment was meant to be a joke, but it had a serious layer to it too. Julie and her partner had split about a year ago, and it had been touch and go whether she'd be able to keep fostering. She must have found looking after three kids difficult without support, but I never heard her complain. Still, I hated making things harder for her. I opened my mouth to explain what I'd meant, but then Julie said, 'Don't let this distract you.'

Something about the way she said it annoyed me. 'From what? It's summer! It's not like I'm doing much.'

'What I meant was, you've a bright future. I don't want this upsetting you all over again. Talking to the police is all very well, but it's not going to change anything. At some point you've got to accept what's happened, Sophie. Even though it may be hard.'

What was she saying – that my gut instinct that something was wrong didn't matter? I wasn't in denial about Dani dying – I was just trying to get to the truth. This is the problem when you're 'troubled'; everything you do is put under a microscope. People think they have the right to psychoanalyse you and draw conclusions.

'My head's screwed firmly on, Julie – don't you worry about that. I'm not going to go off the rails, like my mum did – like everyone's saying Dani did! And you know something? It'd be easier to get on with my life if people stopped bringing up my past every time I do something they don't agree with!'

Julie flinched. After a pause she said, 'Noted. Calm down. I can understand that this has been a tough time. You know if you want to talk to me I'm here.'

She went through into the kitchen, and I heard the kettle begin to boil. I felt a bit bad for sounding off, but not quite bad enough to apologize and explain, which I knew was what she wanted. Julie was always concerned that I didn't talk to her enough, and she often wrongly assumed things – like that I was in a bad mood when I wasn't. This would invariably lead to her asking lots of questions and eventually me snapping at her, which she then took as proof that I had been in a bad mood after all.

★

That evening I sat in front of Edith, staring at the chat function on Facebook. Though we hadn't arranged it, I sort of knew Reece was going to come online. When I saw him appear, I opened a message box.

Hey, I typed. *Seen the police yet?*

Yuppers. The charming DI Perry and his anaemic sidekick. They could make a really good low-budget TV cop show.

Ha ha, true. So what happened?

Just told them the facts. Think Mum quite fancied Perry. She wasn't exactly chuffed about seeing the police, but she cheered up when we got in there. Kinda gross.

Ewww! BAD mental images!

Dunno how seriously they were taking it TBH. Figure they'll speak to Anderson. Dunno if much else will happen.

Or if they'll even fill us in. This sucks.

But it turned out I was wrong. Just three days later, DI Perry had an update for me.

REECE

When I'd finished chatting to Sophie online I went downstairs to get a drink. Mum was in the kitchen watering the pot plants. Though I'd been joking about her fancying DI Perry, it was making me wonder how I'd feel if Mum did start seeing someone. It wasn't impossible. She wasn't that ancient, and compared to some of my mates' mothers, she looked pretty good. And she was lonely – I'd heard her complaining to Aunt Meg. It couldn't be much fun just looking after Neve. Mum didn't even meet people through a job. Thanks to Dad's life-insurance payout she could afford not to work.

It was over three years now since Dad had died, and I missed him like it had happened yesterday. It was particularly bad whenever I saw my mates' dads cheering them on at cricket matches, because I knew how much Dad would have enjoyed that. Whenever I thought about him too long all kinds of questions rolled through my mind. What would he think of how I'd turned out? Would I be different if he was still here?

I guessed what Sophie was feeling now wasn't so very different, even though Danielle had been in and out of her life while Dad had been in mine every day. It was a colossal blow to lose someone you cared about, and she'd already lost her mum before Dani. How had I lost sight of that? I made up my mind to be a better friend to her.

'What are you doing tomorrow?' Mum asked as I took a can of Coke from the fridge.

I made a non-committal noise. 'Go over to Sophie's maybe. Talk over the police thing.'

Mum didn't look surprised. 'Don't get too caught up in this, Reece. That girl drags you down.'

'What do you mean?'

Mum brushed a droplet of water off a peace-lily petal. 'I don't know Sophie well, but I can't imagine she's a particularly easy friend to have. You've gone out of your way to support her in the past, and I'm not sure how much you get back. It seems to me that Sophie only wants you around when she needs you.'

'You're wrong. What about when Dad died?'

Mum looked away, and I regretted bringing it up.

You always hear that when something terrible happens the only upside is that it brings people together. That certainly happened for me, but it had been Sophie I'd got closer to, not Mum. Mum had been seven months pregnant with Neve when Dad died, and she was all over the place. Frankly she'd scared me.

Part of me thinks Mum's never forgiven Sophie for the fact that I turned to *her*. And part of me thinks Mum's never forgiven herself.

'Sorry,' I muttered. The word hung in the air. I wasn't sure whether or not Mum heard. She went on watering the plants.

SOPHIE

I ran into the park, feeling like my lungs were burning. A quick glance told me that Paloma and co. weren't sunning themselves in their usual spot. No one could get at me or ask any awkward questions. I slowed down, my breathing returning to normal. There was an empty swing in the play area so I claimed it and swung higher, higher, higher, until I started to feel heady.

I'd been so hopeful an hour ago when Julie and I had gone back to the police station. When Perry and Grace appeared, Perry's first words were, 'We've spoken to Mr Anderson.'

'Did you find him easily?' I asked, trying not to show how eager I was.

Perry nodded. 'He was rather apologetic he hadn't come to us before. He admits that he saw Danielle the weekend she died – in town and at the flat. According to him, they'd ended their relationship about a month previously. That morning in town had been the first time they'd seen each other since – hence Danielle's reaction. He hadn't known she was in Bournemouth until he'd seen her make an online status update referencing it.'

'Right,' I said. Suddenly I wasn't liking Perry's relaxed manner.

'When he called the next day they went for a walk and

a talk, and Mr Anderson admits that he may have upset Danielle. After twenty minutes they parted company, and Mr Anderson drove back to London. We've checked that story, and it's watertight. He stopped to buy petrol on the M3 and we've seen the timed receipt for the transaction. The timing fits perfectly.' He paused. 'It means he was gone by the time Danielle died. At best he's only indirectly involved with her death.'

I stared at him.

Perry continued. 'I understand that your cousin seemed happy that weekend, but the facts still stand: she did have mood swings, she hadn't been taking her medication, she suffered from depression and she'd split with her boyfriend. All this is painting a bit of a picture, wouldn't you say?'

Perry and Grace looked at me expectantly, as though awaiting me to congratulate them on their stellar detective work.

'That's it?' I blurted. 'Case closed?'

'Sophie,' Perry said, 'I understand that this is upsetting. But you have to trust our judgement and let it go.'

'This makes it Anderson's fault though, doesn't it? He's the one who upset her that day – isn't he going to get into trouble?'

'He hasn't committed a crime, Sophie,' Julie said softly. 'I think you have to accept the facts—'

'No, I don't.' I stood, causing the chair legs to screech

on the tiled floor. Julie laid a hand on my arm, but I shook her off. I didn't care if I was being rude. It wasn't as simple as Dani being depressed! I'd told them she wasn't like that. And what about her going off the balcony backwards?

My head was spinning. I needed to be alone. I thought someone, probably Julie, would stop me as I stormed out, but I heard Perry say, 'Let her go; she'll calm down.' Patronizing git – all the time pretending he understood when he'd clearly thought I was crazy, just like my mum and cousin!

As I mulled this over, sitting on the swing, I became even more convinced that Danielle hadn't just killed herself over some man. She'd fought hard for everything she had – she wouldn't throw it away like that! So what did this mean? That someone had been responsible for her death? It seemed mad, and I could hardly believe I was thinking it. But if it wasn't suicide, and my gut instinct said it wasn't, then it *had* to be murder.

As the swing slowed down and the world became clearer I became aware that someone was on the swing beside me, not swinging, just sitting. A grown-up someone, who shouldn't really be in the kiddies' play area. A grown-up someone who was looking at me.

'Sorry to butt in . . . but you're Sophie, aren't you?'

It was Aiden Anderson.

'It is Sophie, isn't it?' he said when I didn't reply. 'Dani's young cousin?'

He was wearing cargo trousers that stopped just below the knees, flip-flops and one of those silly over-tight T-shirts. I couldn't see his eyes – he had expensive-looking sunglasses on – but his voice sounded gentle. Apologetic even.

This is not happening, I thought. I closed my eyes and opened them again, but Aiden was still there.

'Oh dear,' he said. 'Guess I shouldn't have followed you.'

I jumped off the swing. Aiden held up his hands, looking surprised.

'Calm down! I didn't mean it like that. I left my sunglasses in the police station when I was there earlier, and I was picking them up when I saw you go in – so I thought I'd wait and have a word. I knew who you were – you look so like Dani.'

I took a step backwards. 'Why would you want to speak to me?'

'To tell you I'm sorry.'

I felt a sharp pain in my chest, the kind you get when you suddenly realize you've got something wrong. I didn't know what I was expecting, but it certainly wasn't that.

'I know I have something to answer for,' Aiden continued. His voice had a slight accent to it – Midlands, I thought. 'I'm guessing the police didn't tell you too much.'

I took a quick look around the park. There were several parents sitting on benches just metres away, watching their children clamber on the monkey bars, and there were dog walkers and cyclists passing by. There was no way Aiden could try anything. Slowly I sat back down on the swing.

'OK,' I said. 'I'm listening. But take your sunglasses off. I don't trust people when I can't see their eyes.'

Aiden flipped the shades on to his head. His eyes were very blue. I started to swing back and forth.

'So . . . how long had you been seeing my cousin? She never mentioned you to me.'

'Six months. We worked together. If I'd known she was going to freak when I went to Bournemouth, believe me, I wouldn't have gone. Suppose I was being selfish; just wanted to leave things in a happier place, be friends, something like that. You know what it's like.'

Suddenly I felt very self-conscious. Aiden evidently thought I was older than I was, and I wasn't sure I was comfortable with that.

'You ended up having an argument. That's what the police said.'

'I guess she couldn't stand the sight of me. She gave me a huge slagging off; not gonna deny I deserved it. Dani was really rattled. And then she went back to the flat . . . you know the rest.'

'So it's your fault she died.'

'Me turning up maybe had something to do with it. I'd be lying if I said it didn't.'

He didn't say sorry again, which was just as well. If he had, I swear I'd have punched him.

'How does that make you feel?' I asked in a hard voice.

'Crap,' Aiden said. 'How would it make you feel?'

'Why didn't you go to the police earlier?'

'Why d'you think? If you suspected someone might've killed themselves because of you, would you go around telling people?'

Grudgingly I admitted that it made sense. I felt deflated, like the fight had left me. I kind of wished Aiden hadn't come. He seemed so reasonable. It was hard to hate him.

'Any more questions?' Aiden said when I'd been silent a while.

'Not really,' I said. 'They all seem to have been answered.'

'I'll leave you alone then.' The swing chains jingled as Aiden got up. 'You think of anything else . . . just send me a message on Facebook.'

I heard his footsteps on the soft tarmac and the squeak of the gate. As soon as he was out of sight I realized that I hadn't really asked him anything, but it didn't matter any more anyway.

My mobile buzzed. Reece was trying to call me, and I could see that Julie had earlier too, but I didn't feel like speaking. I turned my mobile off and wandered about the streets with my headphones on. My music player seemed to sense my mood; even though I'd set it on shuffle mode, it seemed to be picking out all the most angst-filled tracks. It was time I accepted it – Dani had killed herself and now I had nothing and no one left. I tried to fall into a zombie-like state and switch my brain off, but it was impossible . . .

Running through my mind were all the times I'd lost people. Not just Dani, but my mum, my aunt . . . and perhaps the most painful memory of all, my 'almost adoption'. I'd been nine years old. The Wilsons had been the kind of couple I'd never thought would go anywhere near me – they had lovely clothes, a nice clean house in a posh area and good jobs, the kind of parents every kid in care dreams of. The bedroom I'd had when I stayed with them on trial was like heaven to me, big, spacious, a lovely bouncy bed and lilac walls – even now I can never see that colour without feeling a little sick. As for why it all went wrong – well, I just wasn't good enough for them. Two months in, they had second thoughts, and that was it. It took me completely by surprise and it's difficult to describe how crushing that had felt. If I'd done something specific wrong it would be easier to deal with, but apparently I just wasn't 'the right girl'.

The really bitter blow had come two years later, when I'd secretly found my way to their house after school one day. I don't know what I'd been hoping to find. The house looked exactly as it had when I was there, except the door had been painted black. While I was standing taking it in, the Wilsons had drawn up in their big BMW. And in the back seat had been a girl, a little younger than me, with shiny brown hair and a freckled, smiley face. She was the new me – but evidently a better version, else I'd have been the one in that seat, with the lilac bedroom and a new chance. I stared at her, and she stared at me, and then the Wilsons said, 'Sophie?' as though they couldn't believe it, and I ran. And I remember thinking, crystal clear, that I would never let myself hope for anything again, because I would never be good enough, however hard I tried.

It was ten by the time I got back to Julie's – by bus, because I'd walked too far to go back on foot. Julie came out of the living room when she heard the front door slam.

'Sophie! Where have you been? I was this close to calling the police.'

'I'm fine,' I said, sloping up the stairs.

Julie reached through the banisters and caught my arm. 'Sophie,' she said softly, 'let's talk about this—'

I shook her off. 'What good will talking do? You think I was crazy to even go to the police about Dani. Leave me alone!'

Julie stepped back, looking resigned. I went to my room. Inside, I climbed into bed fully clothed, pulling the covers over my head.

REECE

I was pretty certain Sophie would have reacted badly to the police's news. DI Perry had phoned Mum and explained about Aiden coming in to see him. It sounded reasonable to me. But I wasn't Sophie.

A freckled kid I didn't recognize opened the door to Sophie's house, probably a new foster-sibling. He told me Sophie was still in bed and bounded off into the living room. I could hear what sounded like a *Toy Story* film in the background. I went upstairs, comparing it to where I lived. This house looked like a bomb site – junk crammed on shelves, children's toys on the stairs, laundry slung over the banisters. It made me realize how used I'd got to living in luxury.

When Sophie didn't answer my knock, I opened the door.

'Hey,' I said brightly. 'Wakey-wakey.'

Sophie rolled over and sat up, rubbing her eyes. The skin around them was puffy and stained with yesterday's eyeliner. It looked as if she'd gone to bed in her clothes too.

'What are you doing here?'

I tossed a paper bag into her lap. 'Elevenses delivery. Full of gooey pastry delights.'

Sophie opened the bag and picked one out, staring at it.

When she didn't take a bite, I said, 'Promise it isn't spinach in disguise. Think that one's custard.'

Sophie put the pastry back in the bag and closed it. 'Don't fancy right now.'

'How about a thank you? That bakery wasn't on my way, y'know.' I perched on the side of the desk, shifting a laptop and some books to make space. How the heck did she cope living in this shoebox of a room? It would've driven me spare. 'Tried to call you yesterday. I take it the police had a word.'

She shrugged. 'It made sense. End of story, I guess.'

'Hey, where's your fighting spirit? I was expecting you to be insisting they'd got it wrong.'

'Maybe I would be, if I hadn't got Aiden's side of the story afterwards.'

She explained what had happened in the park.

'Are you serious?' I exclaimed, leaning forward and nearly falling off the desk. 'The guy followed you? Soph, that's proper stalker behaviour! Are you not even mildly freaked out?'

'Not any more. He was OK.'

'I don't give a toss how OK he was! He still *followed* you.'

'Yeah, but I can understand why he felt he had to talk to me. I wanted to blame him for everything, but what's the point?' She paused. I had nothing to say; I didn't like hearing her sound this defeated. 'For a while I was convinced that someone must have killed her. But it's like Perry said, isn't it? At most Aiden's *indirectly* responsible. Or maybe he had nothing to do with it and she jumped because she was unstable. I'll never know. I should just get over it.'

I shrugged. Letting Danielle go probably was the best thing Sophie could do, but it didn't seem very loyal to say so. Sophie started fiddling with the bedsheets, popping and unpopping the end of the duvet cover. After a moment she said, 'Didn't mean to drag you into this.'

I made a non-committal noise.

'D'you want to stay for lunch?' Sophie asked. 'If you don't mind hanging around while I get up.'

I went downstairs to wait and watched the end of *Toy Story 2* with the kids. After about half an hour Sophie appeared, looking a lot fresher. She gave me a self-conscious smile. We went into the kitchen and shared the pastries I'd brought while she made some ham sandwiches. She still wasn't saying much. I wondered if she felt weird about me being around her house again.

'Wanna do something this afternoon?' I asked.

Sophie looked at me with a slight frown. 'What kind of thing?'

I didn't actually have a plan so I improvised. 'Let's go on the London Eye.' As soon as I said it I knew I'd made a mistake. The Eye would be way too expensive for Sophie.

Quickly I added, 'I'll pay. Haven't spent all my birthday money yet.'

I was convinced that Sophie would refuse. She hated money being an issue. Plus, I was hyper-aware that it sounded like I was asking her on a date. To my surprise she smiled.

'You don't like heights. The Eye's a slow version of a big wheel – you chicken out of those at theme parks. And does the Year 8 trip to Edinburgh Castle ring any bells? As I remember, there was a lot of complaining from you that going up on the battlements was a waste of time – and then deathly silence once we were up there . . .'

'I wasn't scared. I was admiring the view.'

'Yeah, right. Let's go.'

On the tube together it was almost like old times. When we reached the South Bank there was a staggeringly long queue of tourists by the Eye but it moved more quickly than we expected. As we got in our pod and it started to rise, I realized this wasn't a good idea. I'd thought the Eye would be fine because it moves so slowly. Unfortunately I'd forgotten how small the world starts to look when you get up high. I retreated to the bench in the centre of the pod where it seemed safest, leaving everyone else oohing and aahing about the view from the sides.

'Knew you'd wimp out.' Sophie wasn't making any

effort to disguise her laughter. 'Come on, coward, live a little. There's a great view of Big Ben.'

'I'm not a coward. I just have a highly toned sense of self-preservation,' I said, feeling my stomach clench. Good job this wasn't a date. Talk about losing street cred! 'I can see Big Ben supremely well from ground level, thanks.'

'Like I said: coward. What d'you think the Eye's going to do, suddenly topple over and crash into the Thames?'

'First time for everything,' I said. But as we eased our way higher I ventured nearer to the windows. Actually it was pretty cool. We'd picked a clear day and could see for miles. So long as I didn't look directly down I was fine.

After we'd done the full cycle we went along to Tate Modern and mocked the crazy artwork. It was great just to be with Sophie without talking about Danielle. It was, simply, a nice, ordinary day – exactly what we both needed.

SOPHIE

Wednesday was busy. I spent the morning in Save the Animals and then sought out Paloma and co. in the park. We ended up moving on to the milkshake bar. It felt good to be doing normal things. On the way we passed Broom Hill. As I looked at the grey buildings and imagined myself walking back through the doors in a few weeks' time I felt a horrible sense of dread.

It was only when I was making my way home that evening that I had a chance to think about Danielle. Now I'd had time to reflect I didn't feel anywhere near as angry as I had been – just sad. At least now I'd talked to Aiden I had some kind of closure.

As I was walking down the road, digging in my bag for keys, I noticed a blue Mini parked opposite my house. I never normally noticed cars – but I'd seen this one before . . .

It had been parked in exactly the same spot when I'd come back from the London Eye yesterday. I had noticed it because it was one of those new, hip Minis that sometimes have a pattern on the roof, a Union Jack or something. April, the seven-year-old Julie's fostering, has a Barbie car just like it. I had been able to make out the driver's outline and had assumed he was waiting to pick someone up, which had struck me as funny. Our road is mainly full of old people. I couldn't imagine any of them ever jumping into a cool car, let alone at 9 p.m. when they could be home watching *Midsomer Murders*.

So who was it waiting for? Yet again the driver was sitting inside. I didn't have a great view of him – I was approaching from behind – and I was a little afraid of looking back once I'd passed by. Maybe it was paranoia, but something was warning me not to freak out – to act normal. I let myself into the house and ran upstairs to Julie's room. I knew there would be binoculars there – Julie birdwatches every so often. Finding them, I went back into my room and closed the door behind me.

You're being silly, I told myself as I approached the window, from the side, where I couldn't be seen.

The man in the Mini was Aiden Anderson.

My heart began to pump. Slowly I poked my head above the windowsill, still peeping through the blinds. It was definitely him – he was talking to someone on his mobile and he didn't look too happy.

Shit! I thought. How does he know where I live? Followed me again, I suppose!

I drew my mobile from my pocket and called Reece.

'Evening,' he said when he picked up. 'What's up?'

'He's watching me,' I said in a low voice.

'Who?'

'Aiden Anderson! He's sitting in a car parked over

the road. It's creeping me out!'

'What?! Seriously?'

'Do I sound like I'm joking? He was there yesterday too – well, the car was. I didn't realize it was him. What could he possibly want?'

'Calm down, Soph! You're inside, you're safe. Is Julie home?'

'Yeah,' I said, feeling slightly reassured. 'Why's he doing this, Reece? I thought it was over. He explained his story. I accepted it.'

'D'you think he wants to talk to you?'

'No! I just walked past – he could have called out or rung the doorbell or something. He's just *watching* me.'

'Maybe stalking relatives of his ex-girlfriends is how he gets his kicks.'

'Eww – don't even go there! Seriously, what do I do?'

'Call the police?'

As Reece spoke I heard the sound of an engine starting. I watched the Mini turn left at the junction and let out a long sigh.

'He's gone.'

'Good. D'you think he'll come back?'

I had no doubt the answer was yes.

'Maybe I should talk to him next time,' I said, feeling a bit calmer. 'He can't, like, *do* anything. This is a residential road – there are people about.'

'Doesn't mean it's safe. Bloke's obviously a creep. *I'll* talk to him.'

I could just see Reece marching up and demanding Aiden explain why he was playing stalker – in those exact words. 'No, thanks,' I said.

'Did you get his registration?'

That hadn't occurred to me. What an idiot! 'No. It's one of those new Minis though – a blue one.'

'There was a scuffle from Reece's end of the line. I wondered what he'd been up to – it didn't sound like he was out with friends or anything. 'Sophie . . . are you scared?'

'Isn't that obvious?!' I snapped. When there was a silence, I sighed and sat on my bed, lying back on the pillows. 'I just don't understand. I thought this was *over*.'

'Perhaps we should drop in on DI Perry. If I was him, I'd be pretty interested in this.'

'He'll tell me I imagined it! The police aren't interested, Reece.'

'How about you stay round mine a couple days? Aiden won't find you here. We'll work out what to do next. Maybe we can hack into his Facebook account or something.' He cleared his throat. 'This is of course assuming that you don't find the idea of hanging out with me too repellent.'

I hesitated. 'Can't see your mum agreeing.'

'It's my house too. It's not like we don't have space.'

'OK,' I said after a moment. Staying at Reece's wouldn't solve the problem – but it was something . . .

When I told Julie the next day that I was going to stay over at Reece's, she was fine so long as Effie was there. I wondered if that meant she didn't trust us without adult supervision. She didn't comment about us suddenly being friends again though, for which I was thankful.

Effie was less than pleased. When I arrived at Reece's that afternoon she came out into the hall and eyed my rucksack with a sour kind of look. I'd hardly packed much – just clothes, toiletries, Edith, some sewing I was working on – but from the way she acted you'd think I was moving in. She started having a go at Reece as I was unpacking in the guest room, which had an en-suite bathroom and was really spacious, with a double bed and a packed bookshelf. It smelt strongly of vanilla air freshener.

'I can't pretend I'm delighted,' Effie was saying. I guessed she was in Reece's room, next door. 'I wish you'd asked me before telling her it was OK.'

'Could have, but you'd have said no,' I heard Reece say. 'Stop being snobby!'

'I'm not! I just think you're spending too much time with her.'

'You don't like her, do you?'

'She takes you for granted, and what's more, you let

her! And I don't think you having a girl staying over is appropriate. You behave yourself, OK?'

'Mum! That is a total overreaction.'

I creaked the wardrobe door and noisily shifted some books on the bedside table. Reece and Effie fell silent. I let a moment pass, then opened the door.

'Thanks for letting me stay,' I said, poking my head around the door to Reece's room.

'Don't mention it,' Effie said thinly. 'Do you like olives? I was going to get some from the delicatessen.'

'Love them.' I waited for her to leave, then turned to Reece and pulled a face. 'Didn't mean to get you into trouble.'

Reece rubbed his shoulder, looking a bit awkward. 'You know how Mum is. Least Aiden can't get you here. That's the main thing.'

REECE

Mum didn't say much over dinner but there was definitely a chilly atmosphere. Fortunately Neve was completely oblivious and proved a helpful distraction. Sometimes I wished I could get back down to her level. She was nearly always happy. When she was sad, it only took a few words from Mum to coax her out of it. That kind of trust, the belief that people are good and the world's OK – everyone loses that sooner or later. It's sad when you realize it.

I half thought Mum might follow me and Soph when we took our bowls of ice cream through to the sitting room. But she just said something about being in the conservatory if we needed her. I must have been in a strange mood because I asked Neve if she wanted to hang out with us. Neve usually jumped at any invitation to be a 'big kid'. This time she just shook her head. Soph had already gone through. When I walked in she was rifling through the DVD collection.

'I can't believe how many you have,' she said. It was amazing how relaxed she seemed. 'Do you ever rewatch any of these?'

'Sometimes. Any guesses which films are Mum's and which are mine?'

'If the thrillers are your mum's and the costume dramas are yours, I'll have to start reassessing things.' Sophie chose the latest James Bond and we sat down. I stirred my ice cream into liquidy goo, half watching the introduction.

We were very close on the sofa. Though we'd sat next to each other on the tube, on the Eye, when we'd been looking up stuff on my computer, this felt different. Maybe it was because we were doing normal things, rather than talking about murders and stalkers and police. It felt weirdly intense.

I put my bowl down on the table. The ice cream was making me feel a little sick. As Bond blasted villains and dived out of burning buildings, I kept sneaking glances at Sophie. She was totally engrossed in the film. She had always been like this whenever we watched anything, however far-fetched the story. It was kind of cute. Her hair had got really long now, almost to her waist. As usual it could have done with a brush. I didn't think Sophie realized how pretty she was. If she had, she might have made a bit more of herself. Plenty of times when we'd been out I'd seen guys looking at her, but she didn't seem to notice.

Once again I found myself thinking that I could have been a better friend to her recently. It wasn't like I couldn't deal with it – I knew I could. About a year ago Sophie had been acting weirdly. I'd realized something was badly wrong one afternoon when we were hanging out in Caffè Nero. I'd been telling her a story about something funny that had happened in history class, but halfway through I'd realized she was a million miles away. While Sophie might be moody, she wasn't usually like this.

I knew she'd bite my head off if I asked what was wrong in public, so I waited until we were alone at her house. I'm pretty rubbish at this kind of thing, but I must have done OK because she started crying.

'I just can't *think* any more,' she had said. 'Everything's bad.'

'Don't say that.' I put my arm around her. Sophie flinched, but after a moment pressed her face into my shoulder, which really freaked me out. I said a lot of stuff about how it was OK to get upset and I wouldn't tell anyone and how we were going to get past this.

Sophie had said, 'But people don't get past bad things. You think you have, but it always stays with you.'

I had realized a lot in that moment. I'd always known Sophie had had pretty rubbish luck in life. She never bleated about it, but over the years I'd picked up enough to know that you don't bounce back easily from what she'd been through. It messes with your sense of self-worth and your ability to trust. Most people thought Sophie was prickly and had a bad attitude, but I knew better. She looked after herself because she didn't trust anyone else to.

I also suddenly knew that it was really important not to give up on her.

Looking back, I probably should have told someone

at the time, but it seemed like I'd be betraying Soph. I knew now the reason she was feeling so rubbish. A couple of months earlier had been the anniversary of her mum and aunt dying and she'd been to the cemetery to visit the graves for the first time. The loss of her mum had really hit her then. She'd started remembering how her life used to be with her mum, and feeling guilty that she'd been taken into care, as if it had been her fault, and she kept having nightmares about cars crashing. I wasn't sure what to say or that I even understood. I hadn't known I had it in me to be so patient. Over autumn half-term I made her do stuff with me every day and I called and texted when we weren't together. By the time December came she had started taking more of an interest in things.

One day in the Christmas holidays we went to the funfair at Ally Pally and we bumped into some girls from Broom Hill. One of them was Zoe Edwards, whom I couldn't stand. She'd always picked on Sophie in the kind of way teachers didn't notice – nasty comments here and there, elbow pokes when Soph walked down the corridor, false rumours.

'Ooh, we've interrupted their date,' Zoe sneered. The other girls tittered as though she'd said something clever. 'How's it feel to have a crazy girlfriend, Reece? You could do so much better.'

'Is that an offer?' I'd asked. 'In your dreams, Zoe. Why

don't you get lost? Not in the mood for a slagging match.'

'I'm not slagging her off. I'm just, you know, stating the obvious.'

'Whatever,' I said. 'Come on, Soph.'

'Guess it does look like we're on a date,' Sophie said as we walked away. 'They don't get how things are.'

She was talking as if I knew what she meant. Suddenly I wasn't sure I did. 'And how is that?'

Sophie shot me a surprised look. 'You know – mates.'

'Duh,' I found myself saying. My reaction was totally at odds with what my heart was saying. 'What do they know anyway? I want a girl who's shorter than me, obviously – else I'll develop a complex.'

'Yeah, and you've enough of mine to deal with.' Sophie nudged me, and I smiled. As we whirled on carousels and shot at plastic ducks and frittered coins on arcade machines I came to the realization that this 'just mates' thing wasn't working for me. If I was honest, it hadn't been for a while.

The problem was what to do about it.

I still wasn't sure now and it was almost a year on. During the months I hadn't seen Sophie it had been easy to forget about all that, trick myself into believing it didn't mean anything. But we had spent enough time together this week for me to be pretty sure those feelings hadn't gone away.

Sophie snorted with laughter. Bond had just sent one

of his foes flying out of the back of the helicopter, with a typically cheesy one-liner.

'Hey.' She glanced across. 'You didn't laugh. You OK?'

'Uh-huh,' I said, with a big fake smile.

Sophie made a face at me. 'Don't look OK.'

I considered telling her. But what good would it do? The thought that I might be interested in her as more than a mate hadn't even crossed her mind. And I *still* didn't understand why she'd cut me out of her life for so many months. Who was to say she wouldn't do the same again?

SOPHIE

When I woke up the next morning I wasn't sure where I was. I could feel soft pillows around my head and smell sweetness in the air. As I rubbed the sleep out of my eyes, it came back to me. I was in Reece's house, and I'd slept better than I had in a long while. I took my time showering, trying out each of the shower gels in the en suite, posh brands, which, to my approval, were all free from animal testing.

I got out, wrapping myself in a huge fluffy towel that matched the light green tiles, and found myself thinking about Reece's invitation to stay. It definitely showed he was happy to be friends again – generally Reece didn't do things he didn't want to, and he wasn't nice to people he didn't like either.

I heard a knock on the door.

'I am making you Oat So Simple,' came Reece's voice. 'Your presence is required in the kitchen in five minutes.'

'Ten!' I shouted. Quickly I rubbed myself down and pulled on the denim shorts I'd been wearing most of the summer and a lightweight top. After a bit of make-up and a quick hair brush I made my way downstairs. Reece was watching two bowls spin around in the microwave.

'Perfect timing,' he said without looking up. 'The Oat So Simple is nearly fully formed and Mum and the poddling have just hit the shops. Wanna go down the cricket pitch later? I'm playing in a T20.'

'Sure,' I said, taking a seat and pouring myself some apple juice. 'It's been too long since I saw you in action.'

The microwave pinged. Reece took out the bowls, brought them to the table and immediately started swathing his in golden syrup. I opened the local paper. It felt cosy and normal. Aiden and his car could have been a million miles away.

When Reece and I arrived at Berkeley, there was already a decent crowd milling around, mostly enthusiastic parents and petulant-looking siblings, though there were a couple of girls I guessed might be girlfriends. I found a decent spot by the pavilion and sat down, dumping my bag on the seat next to me. I spotted a couple of Reece's friends, but they were too busy limbering up to pay any attention to me.

Reece's team lost the toss and were made to bowl. Reece turned and made a face at me – he was more of a batsman. I waved and gave him a big grin.

About ten overs into the game I heard ringing inside my bag. For a moment it puzzled me – it wasn't a sound I recognized. Then I remembered that Reece had given me his phone to look after before the match began. I took it out. The screen said, 'Mum Calling'.

'Hi, Effie,' I said. 'It's Sophie. Reece is playing in a match right now.'

'Oh. Of course, I forgot.' She sounded flustered. A feeling of unease rose inside me. 'Sophie, listen, could you get Reece to come home as soon as possible, please? I wouldn't normally ask, not when he's playing, but I need him. We've been burgled!'

Having pictured the house turned upside down, when we got to Reece's I was surprised. If it hadn't been for Effie's call and the police car outside, you wouldn't know that the house *had* been burgled.

'Pretty crap burglars!' Reece exclaimed, walking into the sitting room. 'Flat-screen telly – still there! New computer – still there!'

'Reece!' Effie hurried through from the kitchen, a tearful-looking Neve behind her. A police officer followed. 'I'm so glad you're here; I can't cope with this by myself. I came back from Waitrose and found the conservatory window smashed! Sergeant Hill here thinks I might have disturbed whoever it was – they didn't have the chance to take much – but all the same. Burgled! In the middle of the day!'

I looked around. 'Do we know what they took?'

'Your mother's still working that out,' Sergeant Hill said. 'Most of the intruder's efforts seem to have been concentrated upstairs.'

'She's not my mother,' I said quickly. 'I'm Reece's friend.'

'Have they messed with my stuff?' Reece asked, narrowing his eyes.

Effie reached out and gently pulled Neve away from him. 'I'm afraid so. You're not going to be too happy . . .'

Reece ran upstairs, dumping his cricket bag en route. I followed him. As I stepped on to the landing I heard an angry howl.

Reece's room was a mess. The drawers had been emptied and were lying on their sides, his iPod had been snatched from its dock and his bedclothes were pulled across the floor. He didn't seem bothered by this. He was kneeling by the overturned bookshelf, cradling some old books that I realized were his dad's annuals. Some of the pages were ripped and a couple of covers had come off. Reece looked utterly crushed.

'Oh, Reece!' I went over and hugged him. Reece didn't need to say how much the books meant to him – tracking the annuals down had been something Reece and his dad had done together, travelling to second-hand bookshops and searching eBay. Reece had once said that these annuals brought back the good memories of his dad more vividly than anything else.

'Bastards!' Reece said. 'Didn't even nick them. Just tossed them on the floor like they were dumb old books that didn't mean anything.'

'The police will find the person who did this.'

Reece snorted. 'Oh yeah? You got much faith in the police at the moment, Soph?'

I didn't have any answer to that. After a while I managed to coax him into checking what else had been taken. Surprisingly, the only things that seemed to have gone were his iPod and a watch that looked more expensive than it was.

'It's possible the burglar was looking around to see what was here,' Hill said. We were back in the kitchen, sitting around the table with cups of tea. Reece hadn't touched his. I could feel him seething beside me. 'That's quite common,' he continued. 'They take a putty imprint from your spare keys, then return with a vehicle to transport the big stuff – TVs and suchlike.'

'We'll have to change the locks,' Effie said. She looked at me. 'The bedrooms have been done too – did they take any of your things, Sophie?'

It took me a second to realize what she meant. I'd been so upset for Reece that it hadn't even occurred to me to check the spare room.

'Better have a look,' I said, getting up.

I was fully expecting to find the room as I'd left it. To

my astonishment, it was just as bad as Reece's. What kind of burglar does the spare room? I thought, opening the wardrobe. My clothes were all there. Next I checked the bedside table. My sewing – check, make-up bag – check. The necklace and earrings I'd taken off last night and not had time to put on this morning were gone. Weird – I would have thought it was obvious they were just cheapies. Wait . . . Edith. Where was Edith? I looked in the drawer where I'd put her, but she wasn't there. I tried to remember if I'd used her last night – no, I definitely hadn't. Surely the burglar hadn't nicked an old laptop! I sifted through the room, looking in increasingly ridiculous places, but Edith was gone.

I returned downstairs.

'They took Edith,' I said.

'Edith?' Hill looked alert. His face fell somewhat when I explained Edith was a laptop.

'She's not anything special,' I said. 'My cousin gave her to me. If the burglar wanted a decent computer, he should have taken Reece's or the one in the sitting room.'

'They're desktops,' Reece said. 'Much heavier.'

'Yeah, but Edith's ancient.'

I told Sergeant Hill about the necklace and earrings. He scribbled everything down in his notebook, shaking his head.

'Burglars usually go for the obvious,' he said. 'Cash,

credit cards, jewellery and laptops. But considering he's made off with very little of value, he's created a great deal of mess.'

'Am I allowed to clear up, or do I need to leave everything as it is?' Effie asked.

'Leave it for the moment, Mrs Osbourne – I've got some colleagues on the way to dust for fingerprints. In the meantime I'll ask the neighbours if anyone saw anything.'

'Try Mrs Thatchins across the road,' Reece said viciously. 'Nothing passes that nosey old bat by. She'll love this.' He looked at me. 'So much for you coming here to avoid trouble, eh?'

We left Sergeant Hill with Effie and went into the dining room, one of the rooms that had been left untouched. We sat at the table, looking at each other helplessly. Neve, who seemed to want to be with Reece, came with us. Reece lifted her on to his lap and put his arms around her, murmuring something into her ear. Neve rested her head on his shoulder and closed her eyes. It was a bit weird to see them in cuddle mode. Reece was usually so flippant about everything that when I was reminded that he had a soft side it unsettled me.

'Amateurs.' Reece broke the silence. 'Almost insulting we didn't get the real thing.'

'D'you think they'll be back?' I mouthed. I didn't want Neve to hear; poor kid was scared enough already.

'Hill seemed to think they might.'

'If they've any sense they will be. Funny they took your stuff though.'

'The oddest thing is Edith,' I said. 'Why bother? I mean – seriously?'

'Wonder if they got the wrong house? If I was a burglar, I'd've gone for the Carters' next door. They've got a flipping Mercedes, plus they're away on holiday. Nothing about this burglary makes sense.'

We ordered a takeaway for dinner – Effie said she was too upset to bother with cooking. At one point she said to Reece, 'If only your dad was here!'

Reece's response surprised me a little – he slung an arm around her shoulder and said, '*I'm* here. Before we go to bed tonight, I'll go round and lock up and check no one's outside.'

Suddenly I felt like I was intruding.

'Would it be best if I left?' I asked as Reece flattened the pizza boxes to put in the recycling bin.

'Remember why you're here in the first place?' he said. 'Aiden's not going to stop stalking your house just cos we had the world's crappest burglars round.'

I frowned. Reece's words were making me think. When he came back from taking the boxes out, I said, 'Reece . . .

d'you think this maybe isn't a coincidence?'

'The burglary? What d'you mean?'

'I'm just thinking that strange stuff has happened recently – specifically to, well, me – and as soon as I come here, this happens.'

'Everything always has to be about you,' Reece sighed, but he didn't sound annoyed. 'How could it be? They didn't take anything important. Just a necklace and your cousin's old laptop . . .'

Reece trailed off. For a moment neither of us spoke. I said, 'D'you think . . . that possibly . . . Aiden did this?'

'How would he know you were here? Unless he followed us over.'

'He has been watching my house – he must have realized I wasn't there. A friend's is the most likely place I'd be.'

'It's not a totally far-out idea,' Reece said after a long pause. 'Maybe it was the laptop he wanted the whole time. Could be why he was hanging round yours, waiting for the right moment to break in, which I bet never came cos of all the people going in and out. Hey!' His eyes glowed. 'Did Edith have any of Danielle's old files on her, Soph?'

I knew exactly what he was thinking; I felt a little jitter of excitement. 'There were some old folders in My Documents. I looked at them ages ago – didn't seem to be anything interesting, but I could have been wrong.'

'Not that we'll ever know now,' Reece said glumly.

'Oh, but we will. My files are all backed up!'

Reece's face lit up. 'You're kidding. No one backs up their files these days!'

'You mean *you* don't – I'm more careful. Well, Julie is; way back before I arrived one of her foster-kids lost his coursework when the computer died, so now she backs up all our files. We've got an external hard drive. Everything on the laptop will be on that.'

'Brilliant! Thank you, Julie's paranoia! And hey –' Reece grinned briefly – 'who knows, maybe this is going to tell us more about Danielle? Who needs the police, eh? Let's go – oh, wait, crap. Can't.'

He didn't need to say that tonight his place was here. I understood; it wouldn't be appreciated – in fact it would be downright hurtful – if Reece went running off with me when his mum and sister were scared.

'I suppose it can wait till tomorrow,' I said, trying not to look disappointed.

The next day we set off back to Julie's, talking the whole way about what might be on Danielle's files. Reece seemed less enthusiastic now, but he was a bit tired and not quite awake – Neve had been scared about burglars in the night and had kept him up. It was silly of me to feel nervous, but as *not* looking wasn't an option, I'd just have to deal with whatever we found. Not that there would be anything.

Danielle wouldn't have got involved in anything upsetting to me. But if Aiden had stolen Edith, this proved there was something to my suspicion that there was more to Dani's death than we knew.

The house was noisy when we arrived. Julie stuck her head around the living-room door.

'Hello, you two,' she said. 'Nice time away?'

I nodded. I should have mentioned the burglary, but confiding in Julie wasn't really a priority. 'All OK here?'

'Nothing interesting.' Julie waved her hand dismissively. 'We went to see that new film at the Vue – you know, the one about the talking piano. Not recommended; even the kids were bored. You seem brighter.'

'It's cos of my brightening company,' Reece said. 'I'm the alternative to Prozac.'

Julie raised an eyebrow; she's always taken Reece with a very large pinch of salt. 'Well, you keep being brightening company. This girl could do with cheering up.'

After checking what we were doing for the rest of the day and whether I was coming back tonight (I said yes, mostly because I felt I'd outstayed my welcome at Reece's), Julie went back to playing a board game with the kids. I couldn't help feeling glad she was so laid back – as long as she knew where I was, who I was with and that I was OK, she didn't usually ask awkward questions. She had clearly decided that the police interview was history.

I explained to Julie that I was borrowing the external hard drive and promised to bring it back later. Then it was back to Reece's – the computer at Julie's was too public. Once we were in his room, we linked up the drive to Reece's computer. I located my files, and, with a rising sense of anticipation, opened the folder where I'd stored Danielle's stuff.

'Sure this is it?' Reece said. There were about eight files, mostly Word documents.

'She got a new desktop just before she died.' I clicked on the first, but it was just a letter to a rail company asking them to refund a ticket. We looked through the others. A job application, a birthday card made for a friend, some copy-pasted information about travelling to Spain. Nothing I could imagine being worth Aiden nicking Edith for. Frustrated, I threw my empty Coke can across the room. It missed the bin and rolled under Reece's bed.

'Waste of time!'

'Maybe there were files on the laptop that weren't in My Documents,' said Reece.

I shook my head.

'I'd have spotted them.'

'Hey, cheer up. There are still two files we haven't opened.'

'Yes, but one of them is titled "Thank you letter" and the other one I can't open. It's got a weird file extension.'

Reece clicked on the thank-you letter – as I'd predicted it wasn't worth reading – but I could tell his mind was elsewhere. He hovered the cursor over the last file.

'You won't get anywhere with it,' I said. 'Dunno what it is.'

'Oh, *I* know what it is,' Reece said. 'Just trying to remember where . . . aha!'

Mystified, I watched him get up and rifle through the drawers by his bed. Out of the bottom one he withdrew an iPhone.

'That's not yours, is it?' I said.

'Yeah, but I bought myself a new one for my birthday. This is its predecessor.' Reece waved the phone, looking pleased with himself. 'That file, Soph, is an iPhone backup!'

I stared at him blankly. 'What do you mean?'

He rolled his eyes at me. 'God, it's like you're stuck in the Dark Ages! OK, so iPhones access the Internet, take photos, store emails and messages and so on. You can configure it so that if you connect it to a computer, the iPhone backs up everything on it. Looks to me like that's what Danielle did. If we load that file on to this old phone – we're in!'

I wasn't sure how much sense this made, but then Reece had always been a lot more into technology than me. 'Why do we need your old phone?' I asked as Reece pulled out a lead from the cabinet by the desk and connected the phone to the computer's USB socket.

'If I loaded Danielle's file on to my current phone, it would replace my stuff with hers, and I'm not willing to do that. But it doesn't matter on this old one.' I watched Reece as he clicked about on the screen, presumably configuring the file with the old phone. After a while he nodded.

'It's loading.'

'Are you sure this will work?' I asked.

'Trust me! This phone will be a replica of your cousin's the last time she backed it up on Edith.'

It seemed like an agonizing wait as everything transferred. But eventually everything was ready.

'So,' Reece said, 'shall we have a look?'

The iPhone's display didn't just show texts from other people – it showed chains of messages, so we could see Danielle's replies too. I began to realize just how basic my mobile was.

The most recent text was from Aiden, dated two weeks before Dani died.

Hey Dan. Gotta speak to you, please tell me where you are. Hiding isn't making this easier on either of us.

Danielle had responded, *Get lost! Never want 2 c u again! Wish id never got involved with anything and WISH ID NEVER MET U.*

I reread the message a second, third, fourth time.

'Involved with anything' . . . what on earth could that mean? It had to be specific – the choice of words was too weird otherwise.

Over the next hour we read through all Dani's texts. Many were from Aiden. Most of them were affectionate and she often replied with loads of kisses, telling him she loved him. The only other message between them that seemed less than friendly was one from Danielle that went, *Where r u? Its half past & u said ud b in by 10. just called Carl, said u weren't wiv him all nite. Where have u been? Who r u with?* Aiden hadn't replied.

There were a fair number of messages from me – texts were the main way we'd communicated – and also from a few other people I guessed were friends. The only name I recognized was Cherie – she'd been a work colleague of Dani's. Somehow, judging by how frequently Dani had texted me, I'd expected there to be more messages. Perhaps some had been deleted.

'Nothing!' I said, frustrated. 'This is driving me nuts!'

'Her emails might tell us more,' Reece said, scrolling to the email function. 'If we're lucky, this should log us in automatically.'

The iPhone took us straight into Danielle's email account. A load of messages popped up. One – entitled 'done and dusted' – caught my eye.

From: aiden12@hotmail.co.uk
To: dani_yellow_rose@gmail.com; charlotte11@
whizzmail.com; PS2000@gmail.com

Hey guys,
All going well at Vaughan-Bayard's end. We can
finalize the deal in August. Trials are looking
good. Final results due on the 10th. Patrick,
please confirm the arrangements for payment.
Dani, please double-check about smuggling the
data out of V-B. I don't want any slip-ups.
Cheers,
A

'Slip-ups?' Reece exclaimed. 'Smuggling out data? Doesn't
sound very above board, does it?'

My heart sank. 'There's got to be a simple explanation.
Dani was a good person.'

Reece raised his eyebrows as he clicked on the next
message.

From: dani_yellow_rose@gmail.com
To: charlotte11@whizzmail.com; PS2000@
gmail.com
Cc: aiden12@hotmail.co.uk

Hi, Aiden already knows but I thought I would keep you in the loop. Getting hold of the data is not a problem, and I can ensure no one knows we've accessed it. As soon as A gives me the go-ahead I will get everything sorted.

Dani

I couldn't hide from the truth any more. My cousin had been involved in some sort of dodgy activity with Aiden and these other people. Dani might have been flaky, but her computing skills were one hundred per cent. Clearly she hadn't been unwilling. And it looked as if the result might be worth a great deal of money.

So did all this mean that Dani's death could have been murder after all?

I looked at Reece. He was frowning at a web page with a blue banner across the top. The logo beside it said Vaughan-Bayard.

'Pharmaceutical-research company,' Reece said. 'UK-based, main site's pretty near here. Ring any bells?'

The name did sound familiar. 'Dani worked there,' I said, remembering. 'She never told me much, but I think it was a pretty big organization with a small IT department.'

'Aiden's email mentions things "going well at Vaughan-Bayard's end". Seems safe to conclude that whatever was going on involved the company. He and Dani met through work, right?'

The other people, Patrick and Charlotte, might be work colleagues too, I thought. I opened my mouth to say this to Reece – but before I could speak he said, 'I've just come up with a fabulous plan for what to do next.'

Hearing the smug note in his voice, I rolled my eyes. 'Oh yeah?'

'There is, however, a problem. You're gonna hate it.'

REECE

Sophie eventually left just before dinner-time. When I came in after walking her to the bus stop, I found Mum in the dining room, standing by the French windows, staring out across the garden.

'You OK?' I touched her shoulder.

'The new locks have been fitted,' she said. I could see that she'd been crying.

'Why don't we have a cup of tea?' I said. 'Looks like you need one. Neve's in bed, right? You want to talk?'

'Tea won't make things any better, Reece,' Mum said wearily. 'The past two days have been very stressful. The police don't seem to think the burglars will come back, but still . . .'

I almost told her what Sophie and I suspected but stopped myself. If Mum knew the break-in had been because of Soph, she'd go ballistic. Part of me felt like a traitor; my family were suffering because of a friend I'd invited round. But I pushed those feelings aside. They were pointless. Dropping Sophie in it wouldn't make things any better.

'One day you're getting along just fine, then something happens and you realize just how fragile it all is,' Mum carried on. 'What if the burglars had attacked us? I can't protect you and your sister from something like that. There's only so much I can do – and that makes me feel I'm not enough.'

'Don't say that.' It came out sounding awkward.

Mum sniffed, then gave me a thin smile. 'Listen to me. No point going on, is there? Are you home this evening, or out?'

'Home.' I hadn't given the matter any thought, but I knew it was the answer she wanted. We ended up watching one of her costume dramas. I hated it when Mum went needy like this. It made me miss Dad. And it made me feel inadequate.

At least this coming week I'd have something new to focus on, if the plan I'd outlined to Sophie a few hours ago had legs. When I'd explained, Sophie had cried, '*Undercover work experience? Are you for real?*'

'Wouldn't have said it if I wasn't.' I'd quite enjoyed the indignation in her voice.

'This isn't a detective story, Reece! And you're not a secret agent! Those films you watch have messed with your mind. D'you seriously think you're going to find anything?'

'Might,' I'd said. 'You've got to admit, work experience there would be a good way to poke about. Vaughan-Bayard's deffo a part of this.'

'What makes you think *you* should do this? Danielle was *my* cousin.'

'Use your brain, thicko! Stalker Aiden works there. You want to run into him?'

Sophie had gone silent.

'Aiden would know you were up to something the moment he saw you, but he won't know who I am,' I'd continued, pretty confident that the man wouldn't recognize me from the brief glimpse he'd caught of me back in Bournemouth. 'Once I'm in I can get chatting to people. There's got to be some trace of what they were up to.'

'The company might not do work experience. They might think it's odd.'

'Most big companies are cool with it,' I'd said, though I had no evidence to back that one up. 'It's free labour. Schools always encourage students to use the summer "productively". I can just lie and say I'm thinking of doing pharmacy at uni. I go to a nice posh school and I'm taking sciences next year. They'll swallow it.'

'They'll make you work. It's the holiday. Isn't there other stuff you'd rather be doing?'

'Why d'you always have to look for negatives? It'll only be for a week. It's not like I had plans.'

It was almost like she didn't want my help. I'd felt a little annoyed. Wanting me around on one hand, pushing me away on the other; Sophie was so bloody inconsistent. But then she had had a shock. Never in a million years had we been expecting to stumble on to those emails on the phone. Up until now I'd not believed there had been anything unusual about Danielle's death. But now while it still looked like a suicide, it was clear that she was up to her eyes in something dodgy. I couldn't help feeling hyped up. I'd been expecting this to be a quiet summer holiday – lots of cricket, sun, lazing about and ignoring my school assignments. Now Soph and I were involved in espionage.

After a moment Sophie had sighed. 'I guess doing this just makes it seem . . . well, serious.'

'That's the way I roll, doll,' I'd said lightly, and Sophie had laughed.

'OK, fine. It's a good idea. And I might be able to help you get a foot in the door. Dani had this mate, Cherie, from work – I met her briefly at Dani's funeral. I could contact her and say I've got a friend who wants work experience. She might be able to pull a few strings.'

Cherie had certainly done that. It turned out she was the Head of Research's PA, so had quite a bit of power. That didn't surprise me. Everything had been sorted out more quickly than we'd dared hope. Come next Monday, I'd be inside Vaughan-Bayard.

I wanted to set a good impression on my first day of work experience so I made sure I arrived bang on nine thirty. Mum had been delighted when she'd heard what I was doing, especially about my 'wanting to study pharmacy at uni'. She'd always been worried about my ambition to play cricket at county or even country level in the future, saying that it wouldn't lead to a steady income, and how if I got injured I wouldn't be qualified for anything else. I felt bad about drawing her into the lie but what other option was there? Running a hand though my hair and hoping I looked smart enough, I pressed the intercom by the gate. A woman's voice answered, 'Hello?'

'Hi,' I said. 'I'm Reece Osbourne, starting work experience here today. I've been told to report to Cherie.'

'Oh yes, we're expecting you. Come in.'

There was a buzz and I pushed the gate open. It was then that I got my first proper look at Vaughan-Bayard Pharmaceuticals. The only pictures I'd been able to find online had been of the top of the building, which was about all you could see from the street, thanks to the walls ringing the site. Even the gate was solid metal, preventing passers-by from seeing through. If the thrillers I'd seen on telly were to be believed, pharmaceutical companies had every reason to be intensely secretive.

As I walked through the yard towards reception I studied the building. For somewhere cutting edge it looked quite old and a bit shabbier than I'd been expecting. Still, I guessed it'd be a lot swisher inside.

The polished marble reception was more like it – light and airy with plush leather sofas. Rows of photos on the walls showed serious-looking people who were apparently the company directors. They'd be rocking fun on a night out – *not*, I thought. The receptionist told me to take a seat.

After about ten minutes Cherie arrived.

'You must be Reece. Lovely to meet you; did you get here OK?'

'Er . . . fine.' I found myself tongue-tied. Cherie looked like a supermodel. Well, maybe more a movie star – *way* too hot for someone who worked in a place like this. Her hair was dyed dark red and she wore shoes and lipstick the same colour. She was much taller than me, even without the heels she was wearing. She had a natural authority to her that told me she got stuff done and didn't take any crap.

Cherie raised an eyebrow and I felt myself blush. I had a feeling she knew exactly what I was thinking. She probably had this effect on everyone and was well aware of it.

'You'll need to hand over your phone every morning,' she said, nodding to the security guard standing by the reception desk. 'No one who works here is allowed to bring their mobile on site. You can collect it at the end of the day.'

This was a blow. I'd been planning to text Soph with exciting little updates throughout the day. But there was no point arguing, so I did as Cherie said. I also had to walk through a machine which looked very similar to the ones they used for security checks at airports, presumably to make sure I wasn't taking in anything I shouldn't be.

'I've a timetable for you,' Cherie said, leading me down a corridor with the same floor pattern as reception. The air felt a little damp. It reminded me of the science block in Broom Hill. 'You're going to have a crash course in each of our different departments to give you an idea of what we do and how we do it. We can't really give you any depth of knowledge in a week though. Sound OK?'

'Yeah.' She was walking very quickly. It was difficult to keep up with her. 'I'm thinking of doing something science-based when I apply to uni, possibly pharmacy, so any first-hand experience is great.'

We came to a staircase. Cherie led me up to the second floor and through a door with a plaque on it, reading: 'Giles McIntyre, Head of Research'. She swiped her staff card to get in – most doors seemed to be security protected, which wasn't going to make poking about easy. The room inside had another door leading off it – to another office, I guessed – and a very neat desk, filing cabinets and a water cooler. Cherie poured me a glass, which I gulped down. It was a lot hotter here than it had been down below.

'Now,' Cherie said, settling at the desk and gesturing for me to pull over the seat by the coat stand, 'I don't usually deal with work-experience kids myself, but as you're Sophie's friend I'm making an exception. How much do you know about Vaughan-Bayard?'

I'd done my homework. If I was going to be convincing in my role as a keen future pharmacist, I needed to be able to blag. Luckily, blagging came naturally to me. I repeated what I'd read on Wikipedia.

Cherie nodded. 'Yes, that's right. We have other research centres elsewhere in the UK. We're one of the largest independent British pharmaceutical companies. Most are owned by conglomerates now, often stateside.'

'So do you manufacture things we see in the shops, or is it just research?'

'Research. Once a drug has passed all the trials we send it elsewhere to be produced – that's a massive job in itself.'

'Would it be cheeky to ask what you have in the pipeline?'

'If I told you I'd get the sack,' Cherie said, smiling. 'New developments in our industry can be worth millions. There are no end of rival companies who'd love to know what we're up to.'

'But that wouldn't matter, right? You patent your research.' I knew about patenting from watching *Dragons' Den*. Whenever an entrepreneur came along with a new proposition they'd be quick to point out that they had a patent so no one could steal their idea. A company as switched on as Vaughan-Bayard would be quick on the uptake there; too much to lose. I guessed another company could try to develop a similar formula that didn't violate the patent. However, that'd take time, maybe years.

'You *have* done your homework.' Cherie sounded faintly impressed. 'Yes, we use patents, but only after a certain point in the development process. You can't effectively patent a formula until you know it will work.'

Before I could ask anything else Cherie started explaining the employment structure of Vaughan-Bayard, the range of products they'd already developed and then what her job as PA to the Head of Research entailed. She obviously had a lot of knowledge about the company and everything that went on there.

At one point the office door opened and a man wearing a dark blue suit entered. He had thick grey hair and wore rimless glasses. This must be Giles McIntyre.

'Morning,' Cherie said. 'How was your weekend?'

'Very nice, thank you – went over to Hadley Wood on Saturday with Mike, then caught some rays at Lord's on Sunday.' McIntyre hung his jacket on the hanger by the door, looking at me quizzically. 'Who's this?'

'This is Reece,' Cherie said. 'He's on work experience with us this week. I mentioned it on Friday, remember?'

'Of course; how forgetful of me.' McIntyre shook my hand. 'Nice to meet you, Reece. I hear you want to work in the pharmaceutical business.'

I nodded, but I was more interested in his mention of Lord's – the home of cricket. I'd first gone there with Dad for my eighth birthday to watch England play and I'd never forgotten it. Since then I'd spent as much as I could afford on seeing county matches there. Maybe someday I'd be on the other side of the boundary, actually playing on the field.

Before I could stop myself, I said, 'Yesterday looked like a brilliant day's play. It would've been wicked to see that hat-trick live.'

Mr McIntyre looked startled. Too late I remembered that this was the Head of Research at a powerful pharmaceutical company. And here I was mouthing off to him about cricket.

'Er . . . sorry if that was rude,' I said. 'Just got excited. The word "Lord's" makes something go ping in my brain.'

For a moment I thought I was in trouble. But then Mr McIntyre smiled.

'Yes, it was an excellent day's play – I'm only sorry I can't be there today too, though I do intend to tune in to *Test Match Special* later. I'm ninety per cent certain it'll be a draw though. So, do you play yourself?'

'You bet,' I said, and told McIntyre about my club and our recent matches.

Cherie rolled her eyes and started typing. 'You're meeting Malcolm in the lab at half ten,' she said pointedly to Mr McInytre after we'd been chatting for a few minutes. 'The briefing pack's on your desk; it'll take fifteen minutes to go through it.'

McIntyre sighed. 'We'd best get to work, Reece; we can talk cricket later.'

He went into the other office and closed the door.

'Well, you've found the way into his good books,' Cherie said. 'Dog racing, cricket, snooker – take your pick, he loves them all. Smart move.'

I was surprised by how quickly the morning went. Cherie had stuff to get on with so she handed me over to HR. After filling in various forms and having a health-and-safety talk, I was given a tour of the site. There were certain areas I wasn't allowed to go into. Even the post room required a security pass. We weren't allowed to peek into the labs, though we did pass right outside them. I could hear what sounded like dripping water within. It was all very mysterious. Though my interest in pharmacy was fake, I couldn't help but be impressed by how much went on behind the scenes. Maybe if I never made it in cricket, one day I'd be working for a business like this.

At half twelve I was shown back into Cherie's office.

'Good morning?' she asked, pressing the key command to lock her computer.

I nodded. 'Learned a lot.'

'Good. I'll show you the canteen in a minute – we don't tend to go out at lunchtime. Too much of a security faff, and there's nowhere decent round here anyway.'

'You don't have to.' I'd been secretly hoping to get a

chance for a poke about while everyone else was at lunch. 'Wouldn't want to mess up your routine.'

'You aren't,' Cherie said, and I decided I'd best leave it. Maybe I'd have more freedom tomorrow.

The canteen was bustling. The rows of tables gave me an idea of how many people worked here. As we were queuing, I caught sight of Aiden a little way ahead. He was wearing glasses and work clothes but I recognized him instantly. Good job I was here rather than Sophie. There was no way she could have stayed unseen.

'Word of advice: stay away from the soup,' Cherie whispered, making me turn my attention away from Aiden. 'It's always a regurgitation of the previous day's leftovers. And today's Monday – even worse!'

Once we'd got our meals – a jacket potato for Cherie, and a plate of chips, a protein bar and some cake and custard for me – we went to sit down. To my horror, Cherie headed straight for Aiden's table.

Shit! I thought, quickly realizing the flaw in my plan. If Cherie mentioned to Aiden that I was Sophie's friend, I'd be totally blown! This was such a failure of planning that I wanted to smack myself. How had Sophie and I not anticipated this?

'Hi, everyone.' Cherie placed her tray on the table. 'Let me introduce Reece – he's on work experience from Berkeley Boys' School, thinking of studying pharmacy at uni. He's only been here three hours and he's already charmed the boss with his cricketing know-how. Reece, this is Aiden – he's a research assistant. That's Lottie, who keeps our admin ticking over, and the other two are Leroy and Amit, from the labs.'

'Hi,' I said, flashing them a smile that hid how uneasy I felt. 'Hope you don't mind me gatecrashing.'

Cherie sat next to Leroy. I took the last chair, between her and Lottie. Lottie started asking me polite questions about my school and family. When I said I had a three-year-old sister, she made cooing noises. Cherie, who'd overheard, rolled her eyes at me. I resisted the urge to make a sarcastic comment. This could be significant. Wasn't 'Lottie' short for 'Charlotte'? OK, so she was mousy-looking with one of those droney voices that made you want to fall asleep, but that didn't mean she couldn't be the Charlotte in the emails. She was lunching with Aiden, after all.

I noticed that Aiden had stopped eating. He was stirring rice around on his plate, eyes on me. I began to feel uncomfortable.

'What makes you interested in pharmacy?' Aiden asked when there was a lull in the conversation. His tone was deadpan, impossible to read.

'Chance to help people,' I said. It was the first thing that came into my head. 'Drugs change sick people's lives. It'd be great to be able to contribute to that.'

'It's not all about helping people.'

'Really? I thought that was what pharmaceuticals were for.'

'They are. But it isn't easy. And sometimes, in developing drugs, there are problems. Not very nice problems. Sometimes we get it wrong and people end up worse off.'

I stared at him. Aiden returned the gaze, his face composed and unreadable.

'Aiden!' Cherie said, a reproving note in her voice. 'We're supposed to encourage youngsters, not scare them off! Got out of the wrong side of bed this morning, have you? Go and get some pudding and sweeten yourself up.'

'Just giving the kid my insight,' Aiden said. 'Wouldn't want him to think all this is a walk in the park.'

He looked directly at me. For a moment it felt as though the temperature had dropped several degrees. But then one of the other guys cracked a joke about the food and the mood lifted. I stuffed chips into my mouth, avoiding meeting Aiden's eyes. Maybe worrying about him sussing me was paranoid. He was probably always moody and miserable.

As we cleared the plates Lottie said, 'Don't let what Aiden said put you off. He's normally such a lovely guy. I think he's just a little tense; we all are, with the trial results for the new drug coming back any day now. Aiden's team have worked so hard. If they've got it right, this drug'll have a huge impact.'

This was the first relevant thing I'd heard all morning. I almost couldn't believe what I was hearing. Everyone else was so tight-lipped. Lottie was either careless or a couple of sandwiches short of a picnic. 'New drug?'

Lottie looked suddenly uncomfortable. 'It's nothing.'

Cherie touched my arm. 'Come on, back to work,' she said, then, in an undertone, 'Lottie's a terrible gossip; don't listen to a thing she says. Once she gets talking there's no escape.'

'Back to work' turned out to be Cherie dumping four different trade periodicals in front of me and asking me to highlight any articles about research. Not what I wanted to be doing on a hot afternoon. Still, I'd asked for this. I had plenty to think about anyway.

SOPHIE

I kept checking my phone, hoping for news, but Reece didn't text. It was so mean – he'd promised! I messed around with my sewing kit, feeling increasingly annoyed.

'Where's Mr "Alternative to Prozac" today then?' Julie asked when I went downstairs for a drink.

I shrugged. Then, because that seemed rude, I said, 'Reece is doing work experience this week.'

'Smart boy.' Julie handed me a cup. 'We could look into something for you, if you were interested. Summer's not over yet.'

'What would the point be? I don't even know what I want to do.'

'Who says you need to? Just because Reece might have everything figured out doesn't mean you have to. Very few people really know what they want to do at sixteen. No need to be so hard on yourself.'

Julie had got the wrong end of the stick about Reece's work experience, but somehow the conversation made me feel more positive, and we even spent an hour together online looking up jobs and university courses. It didn't make me feel any less annoyed with Reece though. By the time I set off to the meeting place we'd agreed – McDonald's in the retail park ten minutes from Vaughan–Bayard – I was all set to lay into him. If he was trying to build my sense of anticipation or something, it wasn't funny – or fair. After all, I was the one who'd fixed this up. I'd sent Cherie a Facebook message and she'd given me a ring. We'd chatted a bit about Dani before I'd brought up work experience.

'It's such a shame she's gone,' Cherie had said. 'There were so many things she wanted to do.'

This made me feel uncomfortable. Dani had never mentioned ambitions to me. 'I sometimes think I didn't know her that well,' I admitted. 'Like, if someone asked me what her hobbies were, I'm not sure I could answer.'

'Oh, Dani had loads,' Cherie said breezily. 'Shopping, cinema, soaps, dowsing crystals . . .'

Crikey, I thought. Dowsing crystals? Dani had always been scathing to me about that kind of thing. Evidently I really didn't know her at all. But then, people could surprise you.

It was ironic – I'd been hoping there was more to Dani's death. There had certainly been more to her *life* than she'd ever let on.

Reece was late. I was starting to wonder if he'd stood me up. There was only so long I could sit by myself in McDonald's before it started getting embarrassing.

'Hey,' he called as he came through the door. 'With you in a sec. Need fuel.'

Impatiently I watched him go to the till and pick up a

large pack of fries and a Kit Kat McFlurry.

'So much for keeping me up to speed!' I said as he sat down. 'I've been dying for details! I suppose you were having such a great time I slipped your mind?'

'Gimme a break!' Reece replied. 'They took my phone – top-secret research facility. Only got it back when I left.'

'Oh.' I felt a little silly for getting so worked up – and for convincing myself that Reece would let me down.

'If you're wondering why I'm late,' he said, dipping one of the fries in ice cream, then in ketchup, 'Cherie kept me talking. I was all set to make my getaway, but then she made me a cuppa and started chatting about my supposed interest in pharmacy. Couldn't really scoot. She asked tricky questions – maybe she was trying to check I wasn't spying on them for a rival company or something. My brilliant blagging skills got a proper grilling.'

'Sorry,' I said in a small voice.

Reece pulled a face. 'What for? I'm not mad at you. Anyway, didn't find out too much today, though someone did tip me off that they're waiting for trial results to come back for a big new drug they've been developing.'

Now that was interesting. Surely those had to be the results Aiden had referred to in his email? And could the data Dani had been getting be to do with the new drug too?

I said this to Reece. He nodded. 'That's what I thought. Sounds like this drug could have a huge impact if all goes well. Maybe I should ask Stalker Aiden about it. We had a bit of a close encounter today.'

He described what had happened at lunchtime. I crunched an ice cube and swallowed it, not sure what to think.

'D'you reckon he was on to you? Sounds a bit threatening.'

'Too right. Hardly the kind of small talk you expect the researcher to make with the work-experience kid, is it? But it was cool.'

A deep sense of foreboding stirred inside me. 'Reece, I don't think you should be doing this. I'd hate you to get hurt because of me.'

'I'll be fine!' Reece said, sounding impatient. 'And even if Stalker Aiden does suspect, which he doesn't, what can he do about it? Whisk me down to the labs and melt me in acid?'

He looked up, expecting me to laugh, but I didn't. I wasn't worried about Reece getting into trouble at work – it was outside that concerned me.

'I may have met Charlotte from the emails too,' he continued. 'One of the others at lunch. Calls herself Lottie, but seems friendly with Aiden, plus she's the only Charlotte at V–B. I know that cos I took a look at the company Address Book in Outlook while I was doing a bit of database work on a spare laptop. Lottie's mentoring me tomorrow, so I'll try and find out for sure. Tracing Patrick might be more tricksy. No Patricks in the Address Book. Maybe he's left – or never even worked there.'

'We need to find out what Dani was doing,' I said. 'Until we know what they were involved in, we're not going to get anywhere.'

'Hey, I did OK for a first day! It's not like I had much freedom of movement.'

'Sorry, that came out wrong. It's just frustrating for me, sitting about waiting for news.'

'And that is why I knew you would hate this plan.' Reece scooped up his remaining fries and stuffed them in his mouth. 'Chill, Miss Bossyboots. I'm on the case.'

I smiled, but I wasn't convinced.

REECE

Day two at Vaughan–Bayard started with me bumping into Mr McIntyre in reception. We discussed yesterday's match. It had been a draw, as predicted. To my surprise, he had with him an album of old photos, taken at cricket matches over the last thirty years. I was touched that he'd brought it in just to show me. Some were even from overseas, in Australia and the West Indies. Despite being old, McIntyre was definitely on my cool list.

He also invited me to a barbecue at his house on Saturday.

'I always host a get-together around this time of year for the company as a bit of a celebration,' he said. 'The work-experience students too. I know you're only on your second day here, but I might forget to mention it nearer the time.'

Now I felt flattered. It wasn't often people in authority took to me. Usually I rubbed them up the wrong way. 'Thank you. I'll see if I can come.'

McIntyre picked up his briefcase. 'And if you've got a girlfriend . . . feel free to bring her too.'

Had he *winked* at me? Yes, he actually had. I watched him head to the lift. McIntyre *so* didn't have kids, else he'd have realized how totally cringeworthy that was! Maybe not so cool after all. But this barbecue might be interesting nonetheless.

★

I spent the day with Lottie in a small open-plan office on the second floor. As the building was a research facility there wasn't a lot of admin, but apparently it was still important to know about. I could tell immediately that Lottie wasn't going to be as hard a taskmaster as Cherie. But being with her was exhausting. That yawn-worthy voice droning on and on, fretting about whether the filing had been done. Had Aiden warned her I might be snooping? It was hard to tell.

'In here,' Lottie said, 'we've got the admin team, HR, finance and our press officer. The IT guys are down the corridor. They're really important because they maintain our network, databases and records. We might not have the most glamorous jobs, but without us the company couldn't function.'

I wondered if she ever shut up. Lottie took me around, making introductions and pointing out fascinating little features such as the office snack box (very important, apparently) and the stationery cupboard. I wanted to ask her about the new drug, but after the office intro Lottie decided it was coffee time. I'd done some research last night about drug development, and apparently it took years. Whatever Vaughan-Bayard were developing would definitely have been in the pipeline when Danielle was here.

After coffee, Lottie asked one of the HR guys to talk

me through record keeping. This turned out to be way more interesting than it sounded. I'd had no idea what a human resources manager even did. Not only did they keep tabs on everyone in the company, but apparently they conducted interviews, set policies, delivered training and investigated complaints. I quickly realized this might be a good opportunity.

'My mate's cousin used to work here,' I said. 'Danielle Hayward – did you know her?'

'A little, yeah. Really sad what happened to her.'

I decided to chance my arm. 'What was she like?'

I thought that question might raise a few eyebrows, but the man didn't so much as blink. 'Didn't work directly with her, but she was always nice and friendly. Happy to give people a hand with computer problems. Messed us about by leaving so suddenly, but it seems off to speak ill of the dead.'

'Talking about Danielle?' A woman at the next desk leaned across. She looked the type who liked to gossip. She'd stopped typing the moment Danielle's name had come up, so I knew she'd been listening. 'She was all over the place, that last day at work. Really stressed. Jumped sky high when I wanted to clear some forms with her.'

The woman paused, glancing over her shoulder. 'I reckon she must have annoyed Aiden in some way. He came stomping in here black as thunder about an hour after she'd gone, furious about something. Nice guy, but such a drama queen! I do wonder if those two had something going on, y'know.'

The man I was with started to look uneasy. The gossipy woman opened her mouth to continue. Then her phone rang and the moment was gone.

This isn't looking good for Aiden, I thought. The more I hear, the more obvious it is he's up to his eyeballs in something. Maybe Danielle screwed up and knew he'd be after her unless she got out.

The big question was, what were they doing that had such high stakes? They'd evidently not been found out, else Aiden wouldn't still be at Vaughan-Bayard. That made it likely that whatever they were doing hadn't been completed yet. Stealing Edith made a lot of sense. Aiden must have been really afraid that Danielle's files might expose him.

I absolutely had to get closer to Aiden while I was here. It was the only way I could see us getting to the truth.

It was Thursday lunchtime, so I had one and a half days left at V–B. I was running out of time.

Snooping wasn't the walk in the park I'd thought it'd be. I was with people all the time, and most doors needed security passes to get through, and everyone went to lunch together, so there wasn't ever an opportunity to slip off. I had however had a look at the labs. Mr McIntyre had asked me to help him carry some files across there. Thanks to that visit I'd discovered that Aiden had a desk in an office next to the labs for when he needed to use a computer. I knew from my session with the IT guys that all emails were strictly monitored, but Aiden's desk would be worth checking out.

Sophie and I had even hatched an action plan.

'Best chance is lunchtime,' she'd said last night. We'd been at her house, sitting on her bed, sharing a bag of salted peanuts. 'You say you've seen Aiden every day in the canteen?'

I nodded. 'Twelve thirty sharp.'

'So . . . if you went to his desk at twelve forty-ish, he wouldn't be there.'

'Yeah. But I'd have to get lucky. There are other people who work where he does. I've seen them in the canteen, but can't say for certain they go at the same time every day.'

Sophie was silent for a moment. 'What you'll have to do is this . . .'

My eyes were on my watch. Time was passing so slowly! Or maybe it just seemed that way because I was in the filing room, halfway along the upstairs corridor between the main office and the labs.

The door creaked and Lottie came in.

'Reece? Lunchtime.'

I took a breath. 'I've only got a few files left. I was thinking I'd finish these and then come down, so I can start something new this afternoon. Seems silly not to.'

'Are you sure? You've been here all morning. You must need a break.'

'Ten minutes.' I gave her a reassuring smile. 'Could you lend me your pass card so I can come down when I'm done? Won't be able to get into the canteen otherwise.'

'I don't know.' Lottie sounded worried. 'I really ought to wait. We're not meant to lend our cards to people . . .'

'Lottie? We're waiting. They'll be out of chocolate pudding if you hang about much longer,' someone called from outside. Lottie looked at the door, then at me. I tried to look sincere and trustworthy. I must have done a good job, because after a moment's hesitation she handed over the card.

'Just this once,' she said. 'I can go down with the others. Finish up and come straight down though. You know the way to the canteen, right?'

Score! I thought as the door shut. It had been a combination of luck and forward thinking that had got me into this position. Lottie had mentioned the day before that there was a pile of records that needed filing. I'd said I'd do it, banking on my ability to convince her to lend me her pass. Actually I'd finished the filing already. It was 12.35 – my big chance.

Quietly I edged the door open.

No one was about. I hurried down the corridor to the office next to the labs, hoping that Aiden and his colleagues would have already headed to the canteen.

Outside the office I paused. If there was someone inside, how on earth could I explain my sudden appearance? Then I heard footsteps. No time to think! I thrust out Lottie's pass. The light on the security lock went green and I stepped inside.

The room wasn't large – three desks, filing cabinets, some cupboards. No one was there. I let out a breath, feeling the tension in my muscles ease. I knew Aiden's desk was the one by the window. I went over, wondering where to start. There were some personal items on top of the desk – a novelty pen holder, one of those squishy stress-ball things – but nothing worth a second look.

I rifled through the folders stacked by the computer monitor. One at the bottom was marked CLASSIFIED – but it was just a stream of numbers.

Disappointed, I flicked from page to page. Maybe these were lab-trial results? An underlined title – one of the few things that made sense – caught my eye: Weight-loss development. What was *that* about? Unless . . . was that the new drug? I knew there were weight-loss aids on the market already, but something that really worked would make millions. I'd seen some pretty hardcore stats on the news about obesity. Apparently one in ten kids and one in four adults were obese. The Department of Health had called it an 'epidemic'. It wasn't just fitness levels that were a concern – being overweight increased the risk of developing all kinds of illnesses.

I shoved the file aside and tried the drawers of Aiden's desk. Locked – but there was a small key half concealed by the pen holder. I tried it and heard a satisfying click.

There was a lot of crap in Aiden's drawers – chewing gum, biscuits, tea bags, postcards, even breakfast cereal – but there was also a wallet and a personal organizer. I stared at them, almost unable to believe my luck. I opened the wallet first. Lunch was free for employees, so I guessed he didn't need to carry it around. Still, what an idiot to leave it here!

I took out Aiden's cards. Some were plastic, credit cards and gym membership, but there were a number of business cards. My dad had had some that were similar. The names didn't mean anything to me though. Swearing under my breath, I moved on to the organizer, opening it up at the diary section and flicking through quickly to the following week. It was standard kind of stuff – Monday 7 p.m. cinema with Carl and Tim, pay deposit, a dentist appointment, Wednesday 7.45 a.m. HJP, airport, T3. 'HJP' meetings seemed to come up fairly often over the last couple of months. As I was replacing the organizer something slipped from it – a photograph. I picked it up. Then I froze. The door had just bleeped.

Acting on instinct, I crouched down under Aiden's desk. I heard a noise as the door opened and the click of heels. They can't see me, I thought. Let's hope they've just come in to pick something up. They can't know I'm here . . .

'Reece,' came a cool voice, 'come out, please.'

Slowly – dropping the photo on the floor – I stood up. Cherie faced me, arms folded.

'Lottie asked me to . . . I mean, I was just . . .' My mind ran dry. I didn't see what excuse I could make. How had she even known I was here anyway? I stared at her, waiting to see what she would do.

'. . . having a nose about?' Cherie took a couple of steps towards me. I didn't back away, though I really wanted to.

'I fancied a look around,' I said. 'I was bored with filing.'

Cherie gestured for me to step out. As I did so she grabbed my arm, her grip surprisingly firm.

'Turn out your pockets.' When I hesitated, she dug her nails into my skin. That really hurt. 'Do it, else I'll have to myself, and that would be rather humiliating, wouldn't it?'

She seemed like a completely different person from the friendly woman I'd been chatting to all week. There was no way I could refuse. I couldn't get past her to the door to make a run for it either. I obeyed, thankful that I hadn't picked up anything from Aiden's desk.

'This is what happens next,' Cherie said, very slowly. Her tone was so calm that it sent a shiver up my spine. 'You are going to go down to the canteen and tell Lottie that you've done the filing she supposedly left you with. You will give her back her staff pass. For the rest of the afternoon you'll do whatever she says. No questions, no snooping. Tomorrow morning you stay home. I'll let everyone know that you've phoned in sick.' She leaned closer. 'And you and Sophie will keep away from Vaughan–Bayard. Understood?'

She knew what we were up to. Somehow, she knew. Perhaps she had all along.

'Are you threatening me?' I was afraid, but stubborn enough to pretend I wasn't. Cherie released my arm. She looked at me for a long moment.

'How old is your little sister, Reece?'

'What?'

'Three, I think you said? There's a picture of you together on your Facebook page, isn't there? Pretty little girl – looks like you. Your mother must adore her. You live in Muswell Hill, don't you? I'm sure it wouldn't be hard to find out exactly where.'

There was a long, significant pause. She knows everything about me, I thought, dazed.

'Leave my family alone,' I said shakily.

Cherie gave me a bored look, as though I was a very

stupid child who wasn't worth bothering with. 'Don't push me. Now get out.'

I stepped into the corridor. As it swung shut, I saw Cherie go to Aiden's desk, no doubt to check what I'd found.

Well, I might have been caught red-handed, but I had found out a few things – especially about Cherie. The photo that had dropped out of Aiden's organizer had been of her.

SOPHIE

'They're totally blagging,' Reece said for about the fifth time. We were in McDonald's; Reece had filled me in on everything. The cheeseburger he'd ordered was lying in its wrapper, barely nibbled. Despite insisting he was fine, he was clearly rattled – normally nothing got between Reece and stuffing his face. And no wonder. Cherie was scary enough when she was being nice – Cherie in threatening mode must have been something else.

'You say that, but I wouldn't put it past them to try something,' I said. 'Come on, idiot, they broke into your house. Giving your mum or Neve another scare wouldn't be hard.'

Reece picked up the burger and stared at it.

I leaned forward. 'Reece, talk to me. If you're scared, I understand.'

'I'm not!' Reece snapped. 'I'm mad at myself for not telling her where to stick it! Bossy cow. Creeping around my Facebook page and threatening me and thinking I'm just going to do whatever she says! Got a good mind to turn up tomorrow just to see the look on her face.'

'God, we're going in circles! OK, you *weren't* scared. But I'm not sure Cherie's threats were empty. You don't need to go in tomorrow, and it's much better for us if Cherie thinks you *are* scared. Might be best to rain-check that barbecue too.'

'Cherie and Aiden . . .' Reece muttered. 'What a dream team. We missed something really obvious there, Soph. *Cherie*'s Charlotte, isn't she? Not Lottie. I'm no expert on names, but Cherie could be short for Charlotte, right?'

Slowly I nodded. 'Cherie – Charlotte – they even sound similar. That's got to be right. It makes too much sense not to be.'

'Cherie must have told Aiden right from the start that I was your mate. They were one step ahead the whole time – and we played right into their hands!'

I wondered why Cherie had agreed to arrange the work experience if she knew we wanted to poke about. Perhaps she'd thought we'd approach someone else at V-B if she said no, or maybe she'd wanted to check us out. Either way, Reece had walked straight into the lions' den.

As for how Cherie fits into this . . . whatever 'this' is . . . She and Aiden are – or were – in a relationship, I thought. There was no other explanation I could think of as to why else he would keep a photo of her in his organizer. Maybe their relationship was secret. I bet Cherie had got in there quickly after Danielle had died. From what Reece had said about her, she didn't strike me as the kind of woman to hang about if she wanted something.

'Let's go over everything we know again,' I said.

Reece sighed. I couldn't work out his attitude – was he

scared, reluctant or simply bored? For a second I felt bad for getting him into this, though it had been his idea to go into V-B.

I took a breath. 'So . . . Dani starts working at V-B. She and Aiden get together. With Cherie and this other guy Patrick they come up with a plan to make lots of money, probably involving some new drug. It involves Dani getting access to some files. Whether she did that before getting out, we don't know.' Maybe she'd been afraid – or maybe she'd realized what they were doing was wrong. I had to hold on to that. 'Aiden had unfinished business with Dani, because a few weeks after she leaves V-B he goes to see her in Bournemouth.' I frowned. 'I wonder why they haven't got the money yet. They can't have, else surely Aiden wouldn't still be at V-B. He'd have got the hell out, in case he was discovered . . .'

Reece sat back in his chair, folding his arms. He closed his eyes a second, then opened them. 'Trial results.'

'What d'you mean?'

'Aiden's email mentioned waiting for some trial results. That's not something they can rush. That's why things are still ongoing and the deal's not been finalized.'

How had this got so complicated? All I'd wanted was to know what had happened to my cousin. And here it was taking me into something far bigger than I'd ever anticipated – something that was scary and real. Drug trials, payments, secret data – I didn't care about any of this. I'd happily walk away if it wasn't for Danielle.

Reece must have known what I was thinking, because he said, 'Aiden didn't kill Dani, Soph. We know this for a fact. We also know that there was no one else on that balcony. If she was murdered, something clever went on.'

I sighed, wishing things were clearer cut. 'I know Aiden didn't kill her. The police have his credit-card receipt. That couldn't be faked.'

'Maybe the service station on the M3's in on it too,' Reece said.

I shot him an annoyed look. 'Be serious.'

'I am! You suspect Danielle was murdered. I'm trying to come up with theories.'

'Stupid ones!'

We glared at each other. Realizing there was no point taking this out on Reece, I held up my hands. 'Let's chill. All we're doing is getting each other's backs up. Shall we call it a day and meet up tomorrow?'

'OK. Half five here?'

'You're not seriously thinking about going into V-B again? Come on! Whether Cherie meant what she said or not, that's just being stupid for hell of it. It's not worth the risk.'

'Maybe I'll make up my mind when I get up in the

morning,' Reece said airily, getting to his feet. There was no getting through to him in this mood, I could see. I hated it when he was like this. Part of me was just a little bit impressed though.

REECE

I went into Vaughan-Bayard the next day.

Mr McIntyre was chatting with the receptionist when I came through the doors. He looked surprised to see me.

'Hello, Reece. Donna here was just telling me you called Cherie to say you had some kind of bug.'

'I got better quickly,' I said.

McIntyre blinked several times, then evidently decided to let it go. 'Well, good. Wouldn't want you to miss out on the barbecue tomorrow. I've friends coming who I think you'll want to meet.'

I bet he meant retired cricketers! I tried to get him to tell me, but he wouldn't.

'Patience, young man. Now, listen, I know you've been working hard all week, doing filing and other jobs we never get around to, and I hope you've found it informative. We usually give the work-experience students a cash gesture, but I thought this might be more appropriate.'

He reached into his briefcase and took out an envelope. I opened it.

'Tickets for the test match at the Oval? No way! Thank you.'

'I know someone who works at the ground – got a good deal. It's not for a couple of weeks, but it's something to look forward to, eh?'

All thoughts of Cherie and her threats were wiped from my mind. 'Chuffed' did not begin to describe how I felt.

'It's amazing,' I said. To my embarrassment I felt slightly emotional, which McIntyre evidently picked up on, as he made an awkward 'ahem' sound. 'Best thing you could've given me. Thank you *so* much.'

I didn't see Cherie until lunchtime. When I spotted her behind me in the queue I felt myself go cold. There was no way I could avoid her seeing me. Sure enough, as I was carrying my tray to a table, Cherie looked straight at me. I froze, fighting to stay composed. She raised her eyebrows – and that was it. When she'd collected her lunch she breezed past as though I wasn't there. Somehow that was scarier than being confronted. A few chairs away I saw Aiden watching, an odd look on his face.

I wasn't really sure what had made me so reckless. When I'd woken up, I planned on staying home. But then I'd thought of Cherie's supremely irritating confidence and pictured the smug look that would no doubt cross her face when she realized she'd won. I bet no one had ever said no to her. I'd show her I wasn't some kid she could intimidate.

And I didn't want Sophie to think I was a wuss. That was hugely important – though going by how pissed off she was when I met her at McDonald's after work, I needn't have bothered.

'Fine. It's brave, but going in today achieved *nothing*,' she kept saying. In the end I left, though I had intended to ask if she wanted to go bowling. When I got home Mum and Neve were doing a puzzle on the living-room floor, right as rain. Later, when it got dark, I got a little paranoid and went to the window several times in the night to check no one was outside. Nothing happened though, and on Saturday morning I was feeling on top of the world again.

SOPHIE

Cherie's threats worried me enough to call Reece on Saturday morning. He was usually up earlier than me – he preferred doing things to lying in – but I waited until ten, just to show I wasn't *that* concerned. He picked up on the fourth ring, sounding irritatingly perky.

'Hey – newsflash! I'm still alive! So are Mum and Neve. Told you it'd be OK.'

If he'd been in front of me, I'd have smacked him. 'Not funny.'

I heard a mumble in the background; Reece wasn't alone. It was probably the cricket guys; he usually had practice on Saturday mornings. Suddenly I felt like I was intruding – I'd just assumed he'd be on hand to hang out today.

'So . . .' Reece said. I heard scuffling and the volume of voices lessened, as though he was walking away. 'Fancy that barbecue tonight?'

I sighed. 'Are you trying to prove how unscared and macho you are? Give over!'

'It'll be *fine*! Mr McIntyre all but said there'd be cricketers coming. I'm not missing that. Cherie and Aiden might not show. Even if they do, they won't try anything on in a crowded place. Stop being such a worry-guts.'

Reece went on at me until I agreed to go with him – sometimes with Reece it was easiest to just do as he said.

And I had to admit I was curious to see the people Dani had worked with. Only a few had showed at her funeral. Maybe someone would be able to tell me something, especially if they'd had a bit to drink.

We met at seven outside Hampstead tube station. When the lift doors opened and Reece stepped out I did a bit of a double take. I'd never seen him looking this smart before – he was generally a jeans, T-shirt and trainers person. As he came through the barriers I said, 'Since when do you do waistcoats and trendy shirts?'

Reece made a face at me. He'd done something to his hair too – sort of slicked parts of it up. It made him look very different – and actually pretty cool. 'Goodness sake, Soph! I told you this was a smart do. Couldn't you have made an effort? Like, even a tiny one? I bet you didn't even change before coming out.'

'Free country.' I felt defensive; while people from school often laughed at my clothes, Reece never had. I was wearing my usual denim shorts, cardi and a sleeveless top I'd sewn patches of patterned material on to. Feeling self-conscious, I glanced away, fiddling with my necklace.

Reece made a sighing noise. 'I know you're into the charity-shop thing, and that's cool, but treating yourself to something wouldn't hurt.'

'When did you become Gok Wan?' I snapped. 'Like what, exactly?'

Reece pointed at a shop across the road. One of the window models wore a yellow-green dress – quite short and very plain apart from black lace on the neckline.

'You'd look all right in that,' he said. Then, hastily, 'Not that you don't look nice the rest of the time. And not like I, y'know, actually *care* what you wear. Just saying it might make you feel good to have a few new things.'

'I couldn't afford that shop,' I said curtly. It made me feel funny when Reece mentioned how I looked . . . not bad funny, but I didn't know how to react. 'Let's go, OK?'

We didn't really talk on the way to the house. I was still feeling weird about the clothes conversation, and Reece seemed a little embarrassed by it too. As soon as we arrived, though, things were back to normal. I knew Hampstead was a posh area, so I wasn't surprised to find that the house was big – three storeys, with a fancy front, twirly railings and even a balcony. The gate to the back garden was open so we headed around the house and came out on to a patio. About forty people were standing chatting, a barbecue to one side. I breathed in the smell of charcoal and cooking meat – it always reminded me of summer. Reece's eyes lit up when he saw the long buffet table, which was stacked with salads, dips, pastries, tarts and a variety of desserts.

'This is a bit of all right!'

A black dog raced in our direction and leaped up at us, rubbing his head against me. Almost bowled over by his enthusiasm, I backed away.

'Hello, Reece!' A man wearing braces and a checked shirt appeared. He took hold of the dog's collar; this must be Mr McIntyre. 'Glad you could make it. I see Mike's been giving you a grand welcome.'

I took me a moment to realize he was talking about the dog. What kind of a name for a dog was *Mike*?

McIntyre continued, 'He's an ex-racing greyhound – used to enter him at Walthamstow before it closed. Made me quite a bit of money, didn't you, Mister Mike? He's retired now.'

'Is he normally this . . . friendly?' Reece asked.

McIntyre smiled. 'Mike loves people – he's very affectionate. But then most greyhounds are – they make fantastic pets, very docile and surprisingly lazy. But where are my manners? I'm pleased to see you've brought a friend with you.'

Reece laughed a little nervously.

I felt my cheeks colour – the way 'friend' had been said implied something else. 'Er . . . this is Sophie. Soph, this is Mr McIntyre. Y'know, V–B's head of research.'

McIntyre asked us what we wanted to drink and fetched a couple of glasses. I sipped at my lemonade, half listening to

Reece and McIntyre discussing greyhounds and cricket as I looked around. None of the people here looked familiar – but then they wouldn't, would they? I'd never really talked to Dani's colleagues apart from Cherie. Now we were here I wasn't sure about this.

'Hey.' Reece brushed my arm. The warmth of his fingers made my skin tingle. 'Graham Heffer's here! He retired from Middlesex a couple of years ago. He was the guy that made a century when we went to Lord's with my dad that time, remember?'

I'd thought Reece might be exaggerating about real cricketers being here; evidently not. Suddenly we were back on familiar ground; I felt relieved. Reece's cricket brain I could deal with. 'What are we waiting for?'

We helped ourselves from the barbecue and buffet and located Graham Heffer at the end of the garden.

Reece took a deep breath. 'I'm dying from an excess of cool right now. Be honest – have I gone really red? Am I going to make a prat of myself?'

'You'll live,' I said. 'Hey, I'll join you in a sec. Going to pop to the bathroom. Hold my plate.'

I made my way back to the house and found a toilet next to the kitchen. As I locked the door I heard a familiar voice outside and froze.

Aiden! It sounded like he was having a conversation with someone very nearby – perhaps they'd stepped into the kitchen after me. I quickly realized what a fix I was in – if Aiden was that close he'd definitely spot me. And I couldn't hide in the loo forever!

For what seemed like ages I stayed where I was. Aiden and his friend were talking about films – it didn't seem like they were going to move on any time soon. But then, just as I was thinking I'd better make a break for it, a mobile phone rang. It must have been Aiden's, for he apologized to his friend and I heard footsteps pass by. 'Hi, babe,' I heard him say. 'Just let me step outside.'

He must be going to the front of the house. I waited a few more seconds, then opened the door. The hall was empty – Aiden's friend had moved on. As I hurried out into the garden, it struck me that the call might have been Cherie. Who else would Aiden call 'babe'? This might be an opportunity . . .

There was an alley by the side of the house to the front. Without giving myself time to reconsider, I went down it. As I got to the end, I heard Aiden's voice.

'No, I can't just give him a ring!' He sounded on edge, the words coming out quickly – quite a contrast to how he'd been a few minutes ago. 'He'll get nasty if we fuss about money again – asking for more is just going to cause ill feeling.' He paused, presumably listening to Cherie. 'But Patrick knows the day the trial results are due. We can't buy more time. It's pretty certain that we're going to have to develop the drug further. The side effects are too much of an issue.' Another pause. 'No, Patrick won't find out! I'm not telling him, neither are you, and Dani isn't around to have another attack of conscience.'

Dani? Attack of conscience? I pricked up my ears.

'Stop having a go at me, Cherie!' Aiden snapped. 'Couldn't this have waited until I got back? Listen, maybe we should get out while we can. This is getting too complicated – and dangerous! If we go ahead with everything now, Patrick's guys will find out we're not giving them the real deal. He's got contacts, here and in Brazil. They'll come after us! Too many people are getting their fingers burned, and anyway, I don't know how comfortable I am handing over something that has serious side effects. Look, now's not the time to talk about this, I've got to get back outside. Later, OK?'

Quickly I backed down the alley to the garden. More people had arrived while I'd been busy – which was just as well, as it was easier to lose myself in the crowd. I found Reece still talking to Graham Heffer. His food was untouched, indicating he'd been talking non-stop, and he appeared to have dumped my plate somewhere.

I didn't waste time being polite. As soon as I was near enough I elbowed Reece in the ribs, cutting him off mid-sentence. 'Need to talk to you.'

Reece shot me an annoyed look. 'Not now! I'm telling

Graham about the match-winning fifty-four I made against St Anne's High!'

'Excuse me,' Heffer said. 'Just seen someone I know. Nice talking to you.'

He brushed past, waving at someone up by the house. Reece started following but I stopped him.

'Reece, I wasn't kidding! Aiden's here!' I pulled him right to the back of the garden behind a large rhododendron bush and filled him in on what I'd overheard. Aiden had mentioned Dani having an 'attack of conscience' – that *proved* she wasn't entirely willing. Maybe that was why she'd run away to Bournemouth. Maybe she'd known about the serious side effects!

'I was right about the trials being significant then,' Reece said. 'Sounds like the results are going to be bad. What the hell is it they're up to?'

'We should go. Now,' I said.

Reece bit into a slice of chocolate tart. Crumbs dropped on to his shirt and he brushed them off; it was such a leisurely gesture it made me want to scream. 'Aiden's probably already seen us. Don't see what we'd gain by leaving. Anyway, it's not like he can do anything here.'

'Reece! This is about cricket, isn't it? You think you're going to meet more players if you stick around. Is that more important than Cherie threatening to hurt your family?'

'Chill, Soph! What's got into you?'

'Reality check!' I wasn't getting through to him; why did he have to be so stupid? 'Enjoy boring more cricketers to death then. I'm off.'

'I'll text you tomorrow!' Reece called as I pushed my way through people to the alley leading out to the road. I didn't bother replying. As I stepped through the gate on to the street I felt fingers close around my wrist and found myself pinned against the wall, staring up at Aiden.

'Don't make a noise,' he hissed. 'I saw you in the garden. What the hell are you doing here?'

My eyes darted over Aiden's shoulder, hoping there was someone to raise the alarm – but there was no one. The street was dead, and I wasn't sure the people at the barbecue would hear if I screamed. I could see Aiden's car, parked on the other side of the street. Terrified he was going to force me into it, I struggled, pulling away with all my might. Aiden grabbed my other wrist. He was stronger than he looked; his hands on my wrists were firm and unyielding.

'Stop it! I'm not going to hurt you.'

'I don't believe you. Let me go!'

He pushed me back against the wall with a force that winded me. 'You and your mate have got to back off, OK?' he said. 'What you're doing's going to get you hurt.'

'Like Danielle?'

Was it my imagination, or did he wince? 'This isn't just about me. There are other people – really nasty people.

They wouldn't think twice about shutting you up.'

'You mean Cherie?'

Aiden laughed. 'You're better off not knowing. Listen –' he released one of my arms. 'Dani's dead. You can't fix that. Leave it there. Look upon this as a friendly warning.'

I yanked my other arm away from him. He took a step back and I bolted down the road, glancing over my shoulder – but Aiden was just standing by the house, watching. There was a weird expression on his face. I didn't waste time working out what it meant – I ran all the way to the tube station. Only when I was on the train, safely heading home, did I allow myself to relax.

I didn't sleep that night. I kept feeling Aiden's hands on my wrists, the texture of brick on my back. Several times I got up and lifted the curtain, convinced I was going to see a Mini parked outside. At half three I went downstairs and made a cup of milky cocoa and sat sipping it in the darkness, trying to get a grip. Aiden had only been hanging about before because he wanted to get hold of Edith. I wondered what he'd done to her – wiped the files and then chucked her in the bin? It didn't seem important now.

There are other people. What had Aiden meant? Was he talking about the mysterious Patrick or were there more? This thing had to go beyond Vaughan-Bayard – and Danielle, for that matter. But what kind of scale were we talking? Brazil had been mentioned – was this an international conspiracy or was that too fanciful?

The milky drink must have worked because I fell asleep on the sofa and only woke when Julie came down and switched on the morning news.

'Too hot in your room?' she asked as I sat up rubbing my eyes.

I mumbled something about not being able to sleep. Julie perched on the armrest and muted the telly.

'What's on your mind?'

Most other girls probably would have told her. But Julie wasn't my mother. It wasn't fair to burden her with this. And I was scared she'd tell me I was being silly or, worse, mention counselling again. In fact, I realized, I didn't tell Julie much at all. She didn't know how much I was dreading going back to school, or even what I got up to when I was out of the house. I'd been living here a year and a half and she didn't really know me, and I knew that was my fault. Suddenly I felt very alone.

'I should get up,' I said, swinging my legs off the sofa.

'Did you and Reece have a falling-out?'

That was typical; assuming the cause of all this was boy trouble. If only!

'Sort of,' I said. 'He's just being stupid. He doesn't get that having a family is a privilege you don't play about with.'

'Maybe you should give each other a bit of space. I was

going to take the kids to the zoo today. Why don't you come? It'd be nice to spend some time together.'

Part of me was tempted. But I knew Julie would try to get me to talk; she always did. It was easier to say no. If Julie was disappointed, she didn't show it; all she said was that if I changed my mind, they were setting off at eleven. Wishing I didn't find stuff like this so difficult, I headed upstairs to shower.

Should I back off, like Aiden had said? But if I did I'd never find out the truth about Dani, and the need to know was interfering with everything now. I was sure I'd never feel normal again – not until I understood.

Before I knew it, it was nearly two o'clock. I went to one of the nearby bakeries and picked up a bag of potato borekas. What was I going to do next? Julie and the kids would be at the zoo by now; it was too late to join them. My school holiday assignments needed work and I hadn't finished sorting through my wardrobe to see what I could give to the charity shop. Or I could ask Paloma what she was doing. Before I'd found that USB I would have been happy doing any of these things. Now it all seemed trivial.

And that was when I knew there was no way I could let it go. It wasn't that Aiden hadn't scared me; he had. But I didn't think I could stomach the alternative.

I took out my mobile. I had a new message – from Reece, asking if I was OK. I slipped the last boreka into my mouth. Things had been weird with Reece last night, but maybe yelling at him had been an overreaction. He was doing this for me, after all – no one else cared enough to do that. I dialled his number.

'Hey,' Reece said. I could hear rumbling and people chatting in the background.

'Hi,' I said. 'How was last night?'

'OK. Another cricketer turned up, but he only played for Sussex back in the eighties and wasn't that interesting. Didn't see Aiden. Guess he left. You OK?'

'Fine. Sorry I had a go.'

There was a pause. Neither of us was good with apologies.

'Well,' Reece said. 'I'm on my way to Brent Cross – if the crappy bus ever gets there, that is. I'm babysitting the poddling cos Mum's got a headache, but if you don't mind playing with the train set in the Early Learning Centre, we could hang out.'

Relieved that my apology seemed to have been accepted, I ended the call. Brent Cross Shopping Centre was practically on my doorstep. My favourite part used to be the fountain in the main foyer. Above it was a big coloured-glass dome which little kids always used to stand oohing and aahing at. Both ceiling and fountain had gone now. Instead there was a stage area where some kind of event was usually going on. It was there that I waited for Reece and Neve.

'Thought you were never going to show,' I said when

they arrived. 'What was it this time, roadworks at Finchley Central?'

'Naturally,' Reece said. Neve tugged on his arm. She was wearing a blue-and-white-check dress and had a little matching bag. When I said she looked nice, she gave me a twirl.

'It's new. Look at my bag.'

The bag had crayons and a little notepad inside, already full of Neve's drawings. After I'd admired them we set off for the Early Learning Centre. The train set covered a huge table in the middle. A number of small children were wheeling them along the track, making *choo-choo* noises. Neve grabbed a red train from the shelf and joined them. Reece picked up a plastic dinosaur and pretended to attack me with it.

'Would've loved this junk as a kid. Neve doesn't know how lucky she is.'

'Where d'you think we go next?'

He sighed. 'The sarcastic part of me wants to say the Disney Store, but I'm guessing you're not talking about shops. I dunno, Soph.'

I told him about running into Aiden outside McIntyre's house. Reece stared at me with an expression I hadn't seen before. It made him look older.

'Why didn't you *say*? Heck, why didn't you call me? I was right there! Did he hurt you? We should go back to the police, Soph – the guy's a creep!'

I wasn't so sure he was right. When I met Aiden on the swings, he'd had an apologetic demeanour – and somehow there'd been a hint of that yesterday too. I'd been frightened, but he'd seemed almost desperate. I was starting to wonder how willing a participant he was in whatever they were up to.

'He didn't hurt me.' I changed the subject. Reece gave me a sceptical look, but he didn't press me. We stayed in the Early Learning Centre until the attendant started to give us shirty looks, then moved on to a couple of other shops Neve liked. By four o'clock we were all peckish, so we visited the frozen-yogurt stand and sat on one of the many benches in the aisle between the shops to eat them. There was a 'Summer Grotto' display on the stage area, which seemed to involved adults dressed up as Disney characters dancing with small kids and throwing chocolates about. Neve joined in and Reece and I sat back, stirring our yogurts. I was about to say I'd pick a different flavour next time when I realized we weren't alone.

'Hi, Sophie,' It was Zoe Edwards and one of her mates. I felt my insides cartwheel. I hadn't seen Zoe all summer – Paloma had mentioned she'd gone away, Tenerife or somewhere hot like that. I'd almost been able to pretend she didn't exist. 'How's your holiday going?'

'Fine,' I mumbled, putting down my yogurt. Why was she acting all nice?

'Been anywhere tropical?'

Reece narrowed his eyes. 'What do you want?'

Zoe gasped. 'Oh, Reece, I didn't see you there! Sorry, I just assumed Sophie didn't hang out with you any more.'

'Why would you assume that?'

'Because Sophie doesn't fancy you.' Zoe opened her eyes very wide, as though it was obvious. All facial expressions were exaggerated with her; she fancied herself as an actress. 'There's someone else you like, isn't there, Sophie?'

Reece glanced at me and raised his eyebrows in a question: *What's she on about?* I shook my head, swallowing. Suddenly it was like I was at school again – all the whispering behind my back, the laughter. My throat was constricting, making me feel like I was choking.

'Leave me alone,' I managed.

Zoe tilted her head to one side. 'Doesn't Reece know, Sophie? Did you not tell him?'

'What the hell are you talking about?' Reece demanded. I saw that his hands had balled into fists; for a moment I thought he was going to hit her.

'Oh, of course. You weren't at the party,' Zoe said in a pitying voice, 'so you wouldn't know, but Sophie had a very interesting time—'

'*Leave me alone!*' I couldn't bear making a scene like this; I pushed past Zoe and walked quickly into the nearest shop.

Reece ran after me. To my relief, Zoe and her friend were walking off sniggering.

'What was that all about?' he asked, catching my arm. It reminded me of how Aiden had held me yesterday; I shook him off.

'Don't want to talk about it.'

Reece opened his mouth – but then he paused and turned around to look at the stage.

'Hey,' he said. 'Where's Neve?'

REECE

I looked around. The Disney characters in the Summer Grotto were still dancing, but the kids who'd been there with Neve had moved on. Forgetting about Zoe, I ran to the stage, pushing through the crowd milling around it. Children in white T-shirts and shorts and pleated skirts and sparkly sandals – but no blue-and-white-check dresses. Telling myself to get a grip, I waved Snow White over to the edge of the stage.

'Do you know where my little sister went?' My voice came out sounding a little high-pitched. 'She was up here just a moment ago. Three years old, dark hair, check dress.'

Snow White shook her head. I looked around at the sea of faces thronging the stage, then scanned the entrances to the nearby shops. No sign of her! Neve must have wandered inside one of them. Which one?

Zara had the most colourful window display. Come on, Neve, I thought, stepping in and craning my neck to see above the shoppers' heads. Don't do this to me. Damn it, she *knew* she wasn't supposed to run off. How many times had Mum told her? But then when Neve was with Mum she never got the opportunity to stray – Mum was always so careful. I was the sloppy one who'd thought Neve was safe on that stage and had forgotten about her when Zoe had come along.

Christ, Mum would *kill* me if anything had happened to Neve! Actually, she wouldn't – *I'd* kill myself!

She wasn't in Zara. Desperate now, I ran into the shop next door and then across the aisle into a health-food store. Suddenly it seemed that Brent Cross was overrun by children. Sophie grabbed my arm when I came out.

'Reece! Calm down. We won't find her if you're in headless-chicken mode.'

'Of course I'm in headless-chicken mode! My sister's vanished! She's only three. I'm meant to be looking after her!'

I must have been shouting. People were staring at us.

'Maybe she went back to the trains,' Sophie said.

Of course! Neve loved that train set. She hadn't wanted to leave earlier. That was where she would be!

'Little idiot!' I said as we hurried along. 'She'd never try this on with Mum. When we find her we're going straight home!'

We entered the Early Learning Centre. Lots of children were playing with the trains. None of them was Neve. I turned away feeling like I was about to pass out.

'Someone might have taken her.' Sophie's voice seemed to come from a long way away. 'We've got to consider that, Reece . . .'

I couldn't speak. Images of Neve walking off with people, out into the car park and away to their houses, never to be seen again, were shooting through my head. She'd been wearing that new dress. Didn't the sickos always go for the cute ones? It would have been so easy, just taking her hand when she stepped off that stage . . .

'We've got to report this,' Sophie said. 'The sooner they get a message out there, the sooner people will be on the alert.'

My arms and legs felt wooden, like they could barely move. I managed to get going. We went up the escalators and along to the information desk, stationed in the middle of the shopping centre. The woman in charge introduced herself as Ann. She sat us down behind the desk and got me to give a description of Neve and explain exactly what had happened. Sophie chipped in with details I missed. It felt like my brain was dissolving into goo, incapable of processing anything. All I could think about was how much I loved my little sister and wanted her safe.

'We're going to have to call your mum,' said Ann. 'Can you give me her number?'

'D'you have to?' I asked. 'She'll go insane!'

Ann nodded, giving me a sympathetic look. Feeling like I was plunging from a great height, I gave her Mum's number.

Ten minutes crawled by. Ann had called Mum and had made an announcement over the PA system, describing

Neve and asking people to keep an eye out. She'd also sent a message round to alert the security guards.

I felt useless and pathetic. Sitting here hoping each second that the phone would ring, just *waiting* . . . If Neve was anywhere in the shopping centre, someone would have spotted her by now. Ann and her colleagues were starting to look worried . . .

And then the obvious struck. I gave a start and looked at Sophie. She was wearing a stony expression which told me she'd already got there.

'Cherie . . .' I whispered.

'She said your mum and sister would get hurt. She meant it.'

'All I did was turn up on Friday! I just wanted to show them they couldn't boss me about!'

Sophie glanced down. She'd been picking the varnish off her nails. Black flakes were scattered over her denim shorts. Softly she said, 'And they wanted to show you that they could.'

Ann came up. 'I know we're waiting for your mum, but I've passed the information on to the police. There's an officer on the way over. Missing children usually turn up very quickly, but I think it's for the best.'

Ann didn't voice what everyone was already thinking. Neve had been taken. Should I tell the police about Cherie and Aiden? They had to be involved. It was too much of a coincidence. Surely . . . surely they wouldn't hurt Neve. She was a little kid! She'd done nothing, knew nothing and shouldn't even be a part of this. But if Danielle had been murdered – Danielle, who was an adult and could defend herself – then Neve didn't stand a chance . . .

I knew I'd have to mention Cherie soon. Neve's safety was on the line. But I really, really didn't want to. It would antagonize Cherie even more. If she knew I'd blabbed, then she might really hurt Neve. Not only that, but exactly what Sophie and I had been up to all summer would come tumbling out. I could see how far-fetched it would sound, and I just knew that Mum would blame Soph. I could hear it now: 'If you hadn't got tangled up with that girl and her issues your sister would never be in danger!'

There was also the much worse fact that I couldn't ignore – that this was my fault for provoking Cherie, and soon everyone would know it.

In a few hours the car park would be starting to clear out. Happy people laden with bags of shopping would leave, with no idea what we were going through up here. Then we'd really have to face up to the facts.

Someone cleared their throat. I looked up. It was a smiling security guard – and he had Neve with him. Unharmed.

Relief slammed into me when I saw Neve. I felt like I'd aged a hundred years while she'd been missing, though apparently it had only been thirty-five minutes. A lady had spotted Neve shortly after Ann had made the announcement and alerted the guard. It seemed she'd simply wandered off.

'I was drawing.' Neve didn't seem remotely upset. 'Lady was nice.'

'Good job someone had their eyes peeled!' I didn't have the heart to be angry with her. 'Never ever do that again!'

'Look at my picture,' Neve said, pushing her notebook at me.

'Not now. I need to ring Mum,' I said, and at that moment I spotted her coming up the escalator, looking in a hell of a state. When she saw me with Neve she froze. Feeling sheepish, I called, 'It's OK.'

The expression on Mum's face said it was very far from OK. She thanked Ann and her team, apologizing for the trouble we'd caused. It was only in the car park that she let rip.

'How many times have I told you?' she cried. 'It only takes a moment for something to happen. I can't believe you were so careless!'

'It only *was* a moment,' I protested, opening the passenger door. 'Some girls from Broom Hill were taking the mick out of Soph—'

Too late I realized that this was totally the wrong thing to say. Mum stared at Sophie. In a glacial voice she said, 'I think you can find your own way home, Sophie. And if you don't mind, I'd rather you didn't come to the house in future. You've done enough damage. If you and Reece still wish to see each other, that's your business, but not under my roof.'

Sophie flinched, but she turned and left without a word. Incredulous, I looked at Mum.

'You can't do that! This had nothing to do with Soph!'

'I think it did,' Mum said, helping Neve into her car seat. 'If you hadn't been distracted by her, Neve would never have wandered off. I'm not harsh enough to forbid you to be friends, but I can at least control who comes into my home. That girl is a bad influence. I've never liked the amount of time you spend together, and enough is enough!'

I argued, but Mum was adamant. When we got home she took Neve upstairs to have a bath, making a big fuss of her. She didn't say anything more, but it was clear I was in for it later. Feeling wretched, I sank down at the kitchen table. Neve's bag was hanging over the back of the chair. My sister and her bloody crayons!

I must have been sat there a while, because Neve appeared, hair wet and in her pyjamas. She went to her bag and opened the notebook.

'Look at my drawing.'

'Aren't you going to bed?' I said, but Neve just pushed the book at me.

'Lady said show you. Look.'

I sighed and took the notebook – and stared, unable to believe what I was seeing. Neve had drawn what was clearly meant to be a lady wearing a dress with very big high-heeled shoes. The shoes were red – and so was her hair.

'No way,' I whispered.

'Good picture?' Neve asked, sounding hopeful. 'Lady liked it. She said draw her. She said show you and Sophie.'

The childish drawing stared back at me. The crude lines suddenly looked very sinister.

Neve hadn't wandered off at all. *Lady was nice*, she'd said. She wasn't talking about some woman who'd found her.

She'd been talking about Cherie.

Cherie must have been watching us all afternoon. When we got caught up with Zoe she saw her opportunity. She took Neve off, sat her down and kept her amused. When the announcement came through, she just handed Neve over and walked away, cool as you like. She'd made Neve draw her and told her to show us the picture. She knew we'd know what she was trying to tell us. It was a threat, a warning that she really did mean business . . .

SOPHIE

I wasn't surprised Effie had banned me from the house. She hated me already – it figured she'd hold me to blame. What did surprise me was Reece appearing at my house later that evening. We went up into my room and closed the door. Reece perched on the edge of my bed, clutching one of my pillows to his chest. He handed me a notepad.

'Look.'

I took in Neve's drawing, realizing at once what it meant. In a low voice I said, 'Crap. This is serious.'

'You said it. Good job Mum doesn't know – she'd do worse than chuck you out of the house!'

I winced. 'D'you believe me now – about Danielle being murdered?'

Reece let out an exasperated sigh. 'I just know this is fricking dangerous!'

'What happened today proves they think we know enough to worry them. Today was a warning – they were trying to scare us.'

'Know something? It worked!'

I sat on the computer chair and spun to and fro, waiting for Reece to say something else. When he didn't, I said, 'They were showing us what they're capable of. We're going to have to be more careful in future.'

Reece stared at me. 'D'you have any idea how

monomaniacal you've become since we started this?'

'No, because I don't know what that word means.'

'Obsessive. Only able to think of one thing.' Reece shoved the pillow to one side and leaned forward, serious and unsmiling. 'My kid sister just got abducted! And all you can talk about is "Where next?" That half-hour was the worst of my life! I never want to feel that wretched again or to let Mum down like that. This was my fault – because I was helping you!' He paused. 'OK, Cherie let Neve go. Next time she might not. Maybe she and the others did kill Danielle somehow. And maybe they'll do something equally nasty to Neve or Mum or one of us! Do you get that? I reckon it's time we dropped this whole damn thing!'

'How can you say that?' I managed to get in. 'This isn't about playing detective – this is about the *truth*. It matters!'

'Is the truth worth getting my family hurt for?'

'That was your choice!' I felt frustration begin to rise. 'You were the one playing it down, all that macho "I'm not afraid" crap. And this isn't about your family – it's about mine!'

'No, it isn't! You don't have any family any more, which is why you're totally unable to understand what being scared for Mum and Neve feels like!'

That really stung – and he knew it.

'Thanks for reminding me how alone I am.' My voice sounded funny – surely I wasn't going to cry? 'Dani might not be here any more, but that doesn't mean she's not important. I'm not giving up.'

'Don't you care that you're putting my mum and sister in danger?'

'That's totally unfair! You're the one who was putting them in danger!'

Reece shook his head. 'Maybe I was. Maybe I was stupid. But I did it because I wanted to impress you! I don't even know why I bother when it's glaringly apparent that you don't give a damn about me. You just wanted someone to help you out, a Watson to your Holmes or something.'

I looked away. 'It's not like that.'

'What is it like then? Tell me, because I'd love to know!'

I got up, wanting to put some space between us. I couldn't take this; we'd argued before, but I'd never seen Reece this angry.

'To begin with I just wanted to ask you about the memory stick . . . then I realized I'd missed you. I'd never use anyone. If you think that, you must have a pretty low opinion of me. And even if you don't want to help me any more . . .' I stopped; it was really hard to find the words. I was terrible at telling people what they meant to me – life was easier when I pretended I didn't care. 'I don't want to fall out again, Reece . . . I really like having you around.'

Reece slid off the bed and stood up, brushing down

his jeans. For the first time I could remember, he looked awkward.

'It's difficult to tell with you,' he said quietly. 'Some days you make me mad because you're so prickly and hard-hearted, and then other days I remember the moments you've let your guard down, and . . .'

'And what?'

He looked at me. I looked at him.

'This has messed with my head too long,' Reece said in a funny kind of voice. He actually sounded vulnerable. 'Oh God, I think I'm going to tell you.'

'Tell me what?'

'Sophie . . .' He took a deep breath. 'Have you taken a look at yourself recently? I mean . . . you're looking really good.'

I blinked. Now I was really confused. 'What?'

Reece shifted from one foot to the other, looking even more awkward. He stuck his hands in his pockets. 'Well, you're a girl. And I'm a guy. And, um, I like you.'

'*Like* me?' It leaped out of my mouth before I could even think.

Reece's cheeks were scarlet. 'Christ, Soph, you must have had some idea! Yeah, I like you. I've liked you for ages.'

I stared at him. I really ought to have realized this sooner – we'd been teased about it enough over the years, but we'd always laughed it off. The idea of someone as brash as Reece admitting to fancying someone, let alone *me* . . . it was so out of character.

Reece turned his head away. 'Guessing from that reaction that you're not exactly overjoyed.'

'I don't know what I think.' But even as I said the words I knew that I really wanted him to leave so I could have some space. It wasn't that he was unattractive. He really wasn't. And I did like him a lot, but . . . I wasn't capable of being someone's girlfriend! I had too much baggage. Letting someone get that close, touch me . . . it wouldn't work.

Without meaning to I squirmed. 'I'm flattered, but I, um, just don't see it happening.' Crap, that wasn't how I'd meant to put it. 'I just can't—'

'There's so much you "just can't" do, isn't there?' Reece sounded bitter. 'You need to get over yourself cos unless one day you take a risk, you're never going to get past everything that's happened to you. I'm going. I'm fed up with all this and I'm fed up with you. Least now I know how you feel.'

I looked away and heard him leave, closing the door behind him. It felt like something inside me was snapping.

REECE

Convinced something bad would happen, I spent the next day glued to Mum and Neve. Mum was still being frosty about Brent Cross and didn't even thank me when I said I'd help with the shopping.

'If you think I'm going to say everything's OK because you've decided to be nice today, I'm not,' she said. We were in an aisle that seemed to contain nothing but chutney; how Waitrose found so many different types to stock was a mystery to me. 'You may well think me getting tough on Sophie was unfair, but I'm not changing my mind.'

'It's not that. I just wanted to make sure you were OK.'

Mum snorted, but when I didn't react she frowned. 'Reece? What's wrong?'

Everything, I thought. I couldn't tell her about Cherie taking Neve, so I mumbled something about being freaked out about the burglary. None of the items nicked from our house had turned up. I wondered what Aiden had done with them – probably binned everything. Dad's annuals couldn't be repaired either. There was a company online who specialized in rebinding old books but I didn't have that kind of money. In a fair world Aiden would get serious payback.

Mum sighed melodramatically and inspected a jar of quince jelly. 'I'm just waiting for the next horror to assail us. Bad things always come in threes, you know.'

'Yeah,' I said. 'I wonder.'

For all I knew, Sophie might be continuing to poke around, putting us all in danger. I was so angry with her. I got her point about truth. And despite not admitting it, I got that what happened at Brent Cross had really been my fault, and I'd antagonized them with the whole work-experience stunt. But surely now we had to get real. I hated quitting, but protecting my family was more important than finding out what had happened to Danielle. They were alive. She wasn't.

But I didn't want to think about Sophie, not after she'd rejected me. It really hurt. For God's *sake*, it wasn't as though I was asking her to marry me – all I'd meant was that we could try giving it a go. After all I'd done for her too!

Well, I wasn't going to ask again. I felt humiliated enough already. All I could do was try to get over her. It was totally sad, but I was almost looking forward to this rubbish summer break being over.

'Hey! Reece!'

I gave a start. A girl was waving at me from further down the aisle. After a moment I recognized her.

'Hey, Paloma,' I said. It wasn't often that I bumped into anyone from Broom Hill. 'What're you doing here?'

'Picking up stuff for a picnic.' Paloma nodded to a group

of people queuing at the till. 'My cousins live around here. Omigosh, is that your little sister? She's so cute!'

Paloma beamed at Neve. Neve looked a bit worried and hurried back down the aisle after Mum.

'Hey, I heard what happened at Brent Cross,' Paloma went on. 'Totally twisted! You must have freaked.'

I was beginning to remember why I'd found Paloma irritating. She was the only one of my ex-classmates who had a gob as big as mine. Sophie had always liked her for some reason – which reminded me . . .

'Hey, I'm glad I met you,' I said. 'There's something I want to know. You know that party you had? What happened to Sophie that night?'

'Omigod! Didn't you see the videos on YouTube? I thought everyone had. OK, let me tell you . . .'

SOPHIE

I'd thought I'd find Waterloo station fairly empty at ten on a Monday morning, but it was quite the opposite. I stood in front of the departure board, scanning the electronic display for the next train to Bournemouth. 10.25 – that wasn't such a long wait. I found a bench and sat and watched people go by. Like all the big London stations, Waterloo was large and airy, sunlight beaming down through the glass roof. I'd read a news story once about a man and a woman bumping into each other here on consecutive weeks; those coincidental meetings had grown into a relationship, and a year later the man had proposed right here where I was sitting, outside M&S. It seemed dead weird that your life could change just like that – and that amazing things really could happen when you least expected.

I wondered how Danielle's life would have been different if she hadn't met Aiden. She'd be alive, for one thing, and being alive meant anything was possible.

After a few minutes my train pulled into the platform. I'd bought my ticket already so I went straight through the barriers and walked down the platform to the furthest carriage; more chance of being alone.

I wasn't sure what I was hoping to achieve. Last night I'd gone over all my options, feeling increasingly helpless. There wasn't much I could do by myself. Aiden and Cherie would be on their guard, so my more daring ideas – following them about, somehow hacking into their Facebook accounts – were out. I knew other people were in on this, but I had no way of knowing who they were. Going to Bournemouth to retrace Danielle's last steps was the only thing I could think of.

I found myself a seat with a table and dumped my backpack on the seat next to me. As I got comfortable a giggly couple in their twenties got on and sat nearby, snuggling up together. I watched, wondering how it was possible to be so at ease with another person. They were so wrapped up in each other that I didn't think they'd noticed me.

I like you. I've liked you for ages. Reece's words were playing around in my head. I took out my phone and opened a photo of us taken at the Christmas funfair at Alexandra Palace. I was bundled up in a scarf and hat, but Reece, who I always joked was impervious to the cold, hadn't even bothered buttoning up his coat – we made a funny-looking pair, especially as it was starting to snow. The photo wasn't the greatest – I'd taken it myself, holding the phone at arm's length – but it brought back that day. I hadn't really been feeling happy – I was far from OK – but I'd started to believe I could be one day. I'd felt so close to Reece, for the first time properly appreciating how he'd stuck by me. How had things got so complicated between us?

I didn't know why I was finding it so hard to take in. When I thought about it, I'd always been the one to joke that we were just good friends. Most girls would be delighted to have Reece as a boyfriend. So why did I feel like I wanted to run away? And why did I find it so hard to believe a boy could like me in that way? I wanted to apologize, but as I tried to compose a text I realized I had no idea what to say.

Perhaps I needed to get my own head sorted out before I thought about Reece. I knew I'd hurt him – but at the same time, how unfair to blame me for putting Neve and Effie in danger. OK, so if Reece hadn't helped me look into Danielle's death nothing would have happened, but I'd never forced him to take risks on my behalf. In fact I'd cautioned him against it. He just couldn't bear to take responsibility, because doing that would make him feel he'd failed to look after them – and that he'd let down his dad.

Being angry with Reece didn't stop me feeling awful though. I should have handled him more sensitively. And maybe I should have told him the truth . . .

I'd been in two minds about going to Paloma's party. It seemed so unimportant after Dani's death. But I knew I ought to show. Paloma was nicer to me than anyone else at Broom Hill and I didn't want to push her away. Besides, I knew she'd invited Reece, so I'd have someone to talk to. I'd missed him too – thanks to his school play, we hadn't seen each other much over the past few weeks.

I spent longer than usual getting ready. I see-sawed between different outfits and eventually messaged Paloma to ask her opinion. She replied: **U tryin 2 impress Reece? ;-)**

I didn't respond to that. I thought a few days back to the evening of Reece's school play. What he'd said about 'looking the part' had been really annoying and made me feel self-conscious, because I *had* been trying to make more of an effort recently. Not that Reece appeared to have noticed – he hadn't said a thing when I'd started wearing make-up when we met up. I'd not been confident enough to wear anything out of the ordinary, but I'd tried a more sophisticated hairdo a couple of times, which I thought looked good.

Did he really not notice how I looked, or did he *pretend* not to? Was I being too subtle? Maybe it was time I gave him a shock. Not that I'd be doing this for him – this was for me. To see if it made me feel that I fitted in better at Paloma's party, and to have the satisfaction of seeing him realize I could make an effort after all.

I'd arrived at the party late – more chance of Reece having got there before me. I'd texted him on my way over, but he hadn't replied. Paloma lived in the nicer part of Hendon – her house was a semi-detached with fancy-shaped hedges in the garden. She acted like her place wasn't a big deal, but compared to Julie's it felt like a mansion.

I had to psych myself up before stepping inside. I'd deliberately arrived without a coat to make more of an impact – I hadn't come this far just to chicken out. While I felt comfortable enough in my denim skirt, it was my top that was making me nervous. It was turquoise and corsety, with ribbon lacing up the back and sequins on the front that I'd sewn on – not the kind of thing I normally felt confident carrying off. I'd only bought it from the charity shop on a whim. I'd tried it out in the safety of my bedroom, but as yet I'd never worn it out.

Here goes, I thought.

I could tell by the pounding beat that greeted me as I walked in that the party was in full swing. From the number of people in the hallway and sitting on the stairs it looked like Paloma had invited the entire year. I tracked her down to the kitchen, where she was mixing drinks. She shrieked when she saw me and crushed me in a hug.

'Sophieeee! You look gorgeous! Wow! What a change!'

I smiled self-consciously, giving my top a tug. 'Is Reece here yet?'

Paloma giggled and gave me a poke in the ribs. She was wearing a pink dress that looked a size too small. Her cheeks matched it. I wondered how she was still managing to breathe – still, as Paloma was so fond of saying, beauty was a pain. 'You *so* obviously fancy him. I don't know why you bother denying it.'

I wasn't ready to admit anything so I just shrugged. Seeing she wasn't going to get a reaction, Paloma said, 'Haven't seen him, but he might have come in while I wasn't looking. Here.' She shoved a plastic cup at me. 'I made mojitos! *Très* sophisticated, eh? My parents had a bottle of Cuban rum in the cupboard. Edie found a recipe; think I've got it right.'

The mojito didn't taste like anything I'd had before – minty and syrupy, with a crunch of sugar and a strong whack of lime. I wandered around the house looking for Reece, but he was nowhere to be seen. Not sure whether to be worried or annoyed, I finished the mojito and picked up another drink from the kitchen. Paloma had vanished. I was suddenly very aware that I didn't really know the people surrounding me – they were all busy with their own friends and I'd never made the effort to get to know them. I sipped quickly, starting to feel out of place. I caught sight of Zoe Edwards out of the corner of my eye, standing by the patio doors and pointing and whispering to her friends. She was wearing a top very similar to mine and looked great – how embarrassing! Realizing she'd spotted me, I grabbed another drink and quickly left the kitchen. What was Zoe doing here anyway? I was fairly sure Paloma wouldn't have invited her – her gang often took the mick out of Paloma for being big.

I let myself out into the garden. Leaning against the wall, I breathed cool air. It seemed like the party had been going on ages – where was Reece? I'd been depending on him coming. I hadn't replied to his texts after the play because he'd annoyed me that night, but it hadn't crossed my mind that he might not show.

Someone coughed. I realized I wasn't alone. To my surprise, it was Finn Jones, evidently come out to have a cigarette. Finn wasn't the kind of guy who was ever alone – he was one of the most popular people in our year, mainly because he looked a lot like a blond version of Robert Pattinson. Paloma had the hugest crush on him and I could kind of understand why. I turned away, trying to be invisible, but he'd already seen me.

'Oh, hi, Sophie,' he said. 'Didn't know you were here. Wow, you look amazing!'

Had I just imagined that? No, he had genuinely complimented me. He was smiling too, showing perfect teeth. I wasn't sure what to say, so I took a quick glug of my drink.

Finn finished his cigarette and threw it on the ground, stubbing it out with his shoe. He came over, still smiling, hands in pockets, the height of casual cool. 'You know . . .

I never noticed how pretty you are before. You kind of slip under the radar at school.'

'Maybe I like it that way,' I said. To my surprise, Finn started talking about the party. I couldn't believe he was interested in spending time with me. It had occurred to me that I might attract some attention dressed like this, but I hadn't seriously expected it, and not from anyone like Finn.

'You're way friendlier tonight than you ever are at school,' Finn said. 'To be honest, I always thought you were really moody.'

'I don't try to be,' I said, reaching up to brush my fringe from my eyes.

'Then why are you? If you don't mind me asking.'

Normally I'd never answer that question. I didn't feel comfortable talking about my life to anyone, let alone a virtual stranger. But Finn was being nice to me, and the mojito was making me feel less uptight.

'Life is sometimes a bit crap,' I said, not meeting his eyes. 'I feel sad and angry a lot of the time, and sometimes I don't even know why. That makes it tough to be around people – and for people to be around me. And those I do feel I can be with always seem to leave me. My cousin . . .' For a second I felt a lump in my throat. 'Well, she understood me. And now she's dead. Sometimes I look at what I have and it seems there's nothing good.'

Finn looked as though he didn't know what to say. 'I'm sorry. That's harsh.'

'I don't have anyone left now,' I said. Afraid I was going to embarrass myself by crying, I dabbed at my eye – and heard a giggle. To my horror I saw that we weren't alone. Zoe and her friends were coming up, holding their phones and laughing.

'Were you filming that?' I demanded, though I already knew the answer. Out of the corner of my eye I saw Finn disappearing into the house.

'An Oscar-worthy performance – so moving! I was having trouble holding my phone straight I was shaking so much.' Zoe paused. 'Poor little Sophie, such a tragic life, no one to confide in, so much pain! No wonder you dress like a tramp!'

My legs were shaking and for a moment I thought they'd buckle. It felt as if I was about to fall to pieces – and then all my emotions turned into burning anger. I had never done anything to Zoe! How dare she pick on me, make my life more hellish, when it was bad enough already?

I realized I was holding the remains of my drink. I hurled it at Zoe. It splashed across her top, and she screamed. Taking advantage of her surprise, I plunged forward and grabbed her phone. It was a swish new pink iPhone, and that was all I took in before I threw it across the garden. It slammed into the wall and clattered to the ground.

Amazingly, it still seemed to be in one piece. I reached it before Zoe could and brought my heel down, hard.

'Screw your video and screw you, Zoe!' I shouted, shoving her away from me. What I might have done next I don't know – because that's when I realized that one of Zoe's bitchy friends was still filming me. Horrified, I ran into the house and out through the front door. No one noticed me – they were having too much of a good time. I took off my shoes and made for home, tears streaming down my face.

On Monday at school I found out that the video of me smashing Zoe's phone had been uploaded on to YouTube. It was all across Facebook too – cleverly edited so it looked as if I was randomly lashing out. What had gone before I'd flipped, with me confessing to Finn how crap I felt, had been cut. Everywhere I went, people seemed to be laughing and even reciting some of the stuff I'd said. I wanted to fade away. It was useless trying to explain why I'd gone for Zoe. Who was going to listen – let alone understand? And I'd thought my life couldn't get any worse.

Not everyone was horrible – Paloma and her friends were outraged, and a couple of others came up to me and said Zoe deserved it. Many people simply didn't care. Finn actually apologized about running back into the house instead of sticking up for me. He was clearly embarrassed, and somehow I knew we wouldn't be speaking again. Nothing could make the humiliation go away.

I kept thinking, If only I hadn't been to the party. If only I hadn't been lonely enough to latch on to Finn like that. This was Reece's fault! He'd said he'd be there – he'd have looked out for me. Stuff dressing up and trying to fit in – I'd only managed to make myself more of an outsider than ever.

To top it all, the answer to where Reece had been on Saturday night was on his Facebook page. One of his Berkeley friends had uploaded a photo album showing a whole bunch of them out on the town. It looked like they'd been in a cocktail bar. Since when had Reece even liked cocktails or looked old enough to get into a bar? Some posh-looking girls had been there too, and a particularly pretty one had managed to get photographed with her arm around Reece. Even though I knew people always got in close to pose for the camera, it stung. Maybe there was something going on with them. And why not? She was gorgeous and obviously liked him – if Reece was interested, I guessed it would make sense. He clearly wasn't interested in *me*.

All of this just smacked home the fact that he had a new life now, one I didn't fit into. It was time we called it quits.

That had happened about three months ago and it still tore me up. I was afraid of starting in the sixth form because of it – Zoe's behaviour at Brent Cross told me she wasn't going to let things be. I wondered if Reece had seen the video clips – I'd assumed so, but now I wasn't so sure. Had I been wrong to blame him for what had happened between us? I had been pushing him away by making things difficult for him with his new mates, and he had sent me texts I'd ignored. He'd hurt me – but now I'd hurt him.

Was it too late to give each other another chance?

An hour and forty minutes later and I was walking out of Bournemouth station. I took in the scene outside; distinctive yellow taxis, people with wheelie cases, zebra crossings. As I waited for a bus to the town centre, I sketched out a plan. It was past midday; I'd get a sandwich and walk to the flat where Dani had died. The friend who owned it, Fay, was back from her travelling now – I'd sent her a Facebook message saying I might pop by. Perhaps being there might trigger a memory; perhaps I might find something, a vital piece of evidence everyone had overlooked, to prove once and for all whether Dani was murdered.

Clutching at straws – but straws were all I had.

It was about two by the time I reached Fay's flat. I could feel my steps dragging as I got near.

I didn't know if I wanted to be where Dani died. Here, so close to where her body had been found, I couldn't hide any longer. For all I'd been talking about Danielle recently, I still didn't think I'd fully grasped the fact that she was gone. I swallowed, wondering if the bad taste in my mouth was fear or lunch disagreeing with me. For a moment I wasn't sure if I could do it. Then I told myself I had to.

I pressed the entryphone by the main door and felt a chill run up my spine as I realized this was exactly what Aiden had done. Fay answered, the door buzzed and I stepped in.

The lift was out of service – it had been back then too. I stared at the sign. It felt eerie, as though nothing had moved on.

Fay was waiting at the door when I arrived. I'd never met her before – Dani knew her from college, though Fay looked several years older. She had a chunky build and very long brown hair, but the most striking thing about her was the pendant around her neck. It was about the size of my palm and reminded me of the engraved wax letter seals used in medieval times. Certainly a statement piece, I thought.

'Hi, Sophie,' Fay said. 'Good to meet at last. Come on in. Can I get you a drink? You must be parched; it's boiling out there. Only mad dogs and Englishmen go out in the midday sun, as the song goes.'

I wasn't sure what she was on about, so I just stepped inside. There was a funny smell in the air which reminded me of the design and technology corridor at school. I went through to the living area. Instantly it swept me back; I could see Danielle at the table by the window, laying out the breakfast cereals, Danielle by the CD rack, telling us about all the albums Fay had, Danielle putting one in and dancing along to it. I could even remember the night I'd slept on the sofa bed, lying on my side, listening to the distant waves.

After a moment I realized things were different after all. It was messier, for one thing, and the shelves were a lot more cluttered, mostly with semi-precious rocks and dowsing crystals. How many does Fay need? I wondered. It's crystal overload here. Dani would have agreed. She might have been a bit of an oddball, but she wasn't oddball enough to believe in this stuff – she never went into New Age shops. And yet . . . I frowned. Something was hovering at the edge of my mind, something that didn't feel right . . .

Fay came in from the kitchen with a glass of lemonade. She went over to the table and switched off a soldering iron; it looked like she'd been doing some kind of metalwork, which explained the smell.

'Good journey?' she asked.

I shrugged. I wasn't sure what to say now I was here. Luckily Fay seemed to understand.

'I've got a few of Danielle's things, if you want them,' she said. 'Nothing much – a hairbrush, some earrings. Wouldn't have felt right chucking them.' She paused. 'Do you want to be alone for a bit?'

I nodded gratefully. Fay went into the kitchen, closing the door, and I heard the noise of pans being moved about.

Slowly I moved around, letting the memories flood back. For one short weekend, so much had happened. Eventually I reached the balcony doors. They were open. I felt a soft breeze flutter over me. I breathed deeply, looking out at the beautiful sea view.

There wasn't much on the balcony – just a few flower pots and a sunlounger. The iron railings around it weren't as high as I remembered – they really didn't seem very safe. Or maybe I was only thinking that because of what happened.

Summoning all my courage, I edged forward and looked down.

Below was the tarmac path that wound along the cliff-side park. Further down it a man was cycling and there were two teenagers with a German Shepherd on a lead. The path was clearly well-used and yet no one aside from one eyewitness had seen Dani fall. At least being in a public place meant her body hadn't lain there for long.

I turned to face the doors and backed away until I could feel the railings against my legs. The eyewitness had said that no one else had been on the balcony when Dani fell – one reason why it had seemed too fanciful to think it might have been murder – but what if Dani had seen something the eyewitness couldn't? Something, or someone, that she'd backed away from quickly. I knew for a fact she'd gone backwards – that had always struck me as wrong for a suicide. But what could she have seen? What could have scared her so much?

In the kitchen Fay was finishing washing up. I placed my empty glass down on the draining board.

'Thanks,' I said. 'I'll be off now.'

'Did you find what you needed?'

I shook my head. The backing away from something was just a theory – I needed to mull it over. 'Did you speak to Dani the week before it happened?'

'Afraid not. I was off backpacking.'

'Do you think she killed herself?'

Fay gave me a sympathetic look. 'What's the alternative? She wasn't careless enough to have an accident.'

To my horror I felt tears of frustration well in my eyes. I made for the door with a mumbled goodbye. Fay caught my shoulder.

'Hey, Sophie. I'm not letting you leave like this.'

I found myself gently but firmly sat down on the couch.

Fay pulled up a chair. 'You didn't just come here to say goodbye to Dani, did you?' she said.

I made a non-committal sound.

Fay leaned forward. 'Danielle may not have mentioned it, but I'm a trained hypnotherapist,' she said. 'That means

I use hypnosis in the treatment of emotional and mental issues – which covers pretty much anything. Allergies, stress, insomnia, you name it.' She paused. 'Including bereavement. So if you want to talk . . . I listen to people's problems all the time.'

That explained the crystals and candles then. It sounded so tempting, and Fay had a very kind face. 'Don't like the sound of being hypnotized,' I said hesitantly.

'It's actually a natural state, but if you'd prefer to just talk, let's do it that way. Whatever you're comfortable with.'

'I can't let go of Dani,' I began, trying to think how I could word this and not sound insane. 'Everyone thinks I'm just being stubborn, but I've got such a strong gut instinct about her death.'

I filled her in on everything I'd found out so far, including about what was going on at Vaughan-Bayard. The only thing I skimmed over was how I'd been threatened. I didn't need her to tell me off about getting into something this dangerous. 'I can't go back to normal until this is settled,' I finished, 'but I don't know what to do about it – only that I've got to see it through!'

The tears, which I'd done such a good job holding back, spilt down my cheeks. Fay handed me a tissue. Softly she asked, 'Why is it so important to you to get to the bottom of this?'

'Because no one else will! They've written Dani off!

I hate her being branded as this crazy unstable person. I *know* she didn't take her medication, I *know* she had mood swings, I *know* she got depressed. But that doesn't explain her death!'

'Is this just about Dani? Or is it about you too?'

I gulped. 'I . . .'

'What are you afraid of, Sophie?'

'That I'll end up like her!' The words came rushing out. Worried I'd gone too far I quickly looked at Fay, but she hadn't even flinched. Very calmly she said, 'And why do you think that might happen?'

'It's a cycle. My mum was really flaky. Dani's too. That was why I was taken into care – my mum just couldn't handle normal life.' I paused. 'When Dani died people made out she was the same, like it was genetic or something. They didn't say – but I know they think it – that I'm going to turn out that way too. Depressed. Unstable. I mean, it's obvious, isn't it?' Bitterness was creeping into my voice. 'Mum, Dani, my aunt, me – four headcases. I do crazy stuff already. It's only a matter of time.'

'You don't feel you've been given a chance to prove you're different?'

That was exactly it; I was so relieved Fay understood. 'You know the worst thing?' I whispered. 'I can rant all I like, but . . . I have this niggling fear that won't go away . . . that they might be right.'

It was only as I said the words that I realized this was it – the deep, dark fear that had been obsessing me.

'*You're* in control of your future, Sophie.' The way Fay said it, I almost believed her.

'It's never just been about putting the record straight about Dani.' I blew my nose. 'See, I'm not that good, Fay. I'm not one of those . . . those gutsy teenage detectives who'll risk life and limb just to solve a mystery. If it was only about finding the truth, maybe I'd give up. Don't get me wrong, I'm scared – but I'm more scared of the alternative. All my life people think they know who I am before they even meet me. I want to find out who I am myself.'

I sank back into the sofa, tired all of a sudden. Fay squeezed my hand. Why I'd told her all of this I didn't know. Maybe it was just because she'd been willing to listen, or maybe it was easier telling a stranger. Saying what I was afraid of didn't make it any less frightening – but it helped me feel less like I was going mad.

I left Fay's feeling a little better and went for a walk along the seafront to clear my head. At about half six I saw that the pier was getting busy; the funfair at the end was open. I wandered along to see what was going on, more on automatic than because I wanted to.

The pier rides weren't up to much. There was a merry-go-round Reece had christened 'the Euro ride' because it was decorated with European flag bunting, a big wheel for kids and several stalls with games ranging from shooting ducks with an air rifle to throwing weighted balls through hoops.

We had such fun here, I thought; me, Reece and Dani. Standing here and seeing the ghosts of better times was so painful that I turned to leave – then felt a hand on my shoulder.

It was a rugged-looking man in his mid-forties wearing a beanie hat. After a moment I realized he was the proprietor of the air-rifle stall.

'Hey,' he said. 'You Danielle's sister?'

For a moment I thought I was hearing things. But then it came back to me. This guy and his wife had been friendly with Dani. I remembered her chatting to them, and me and Reece having a couple of free goes.

'Her cousin,' I said. 'I remember you! My friend argued with you over your game's rules.'

'Yeah, you and Danielle thought it was a right laugh.' He made a face. 'Is he always that mouthy, your mate?'

'Pretty much,' I said.

The man introduced himself as Jed. 'You're probably bored with people saying this, but I'm really sorry about Danielle,' he said. 'Couldn't believe it. She was only a kid.'

I shrugged. 'Yeah.'

Jed gave me a look, and I had the feeling that he was

weighing up whether to tell me something. I waited. After a long pause Jed said, 'We only knew her for a few weeks, but we liked your cousin, the wife and me. Felt a bit sorry for her.'

'Why was that?'

'Didn't strike me as happy. Not that I knew the full of it, but she chatted to us quite a bit.'

That sounded like Danielle, latching on to people. I glanced over my shoulder, then back at Jed. 'Did she seem . . . scared to you?'

'I was wondering if you were going to ask that.'

Canned music blasted out; the Euro ride had started up again. Jed and I moved to the pier side, where we didn't have to shout.

'She *was* scared − looking-over-your-shoulder scared,' he said. 'She'd got into some kind of trouble and she was worried she was going to be caught.'

'Please . . . you've got to tell me everything you know. It's important.'

He gave me a long look. 'Exactly what she did I don't know, but she said she'd got hold of some information she wasn't supposed to have. Information she thought might be dangerous.'

'Did she mention Aiden at all? Her ex?'

'Yeah. She was obviously really upset about them breaking up. Kept calling him a cheating bastard. She seemed to blame him for everything.'

I took this in, rearranging the dynamics between Dani and Aiden in my head. So he'd roped her into this – and he'd cheated on her too? It had to be with Cherie. I bet Dani had wanted nothing further to do with him – or what he'd asked her to do. Maybe that was why she'd quit her job and run away.

'Not much more I can tell you.' Jed's eyes were on his stand. 'But she did say she needed to make a decision – whether to speak up or shut up – and I don't know which she chose. The local paper said it was suicide, but me and the wife didn't believe it. Doesn't tally.'

I thanked Jed and let him get back to work. He'd given me a lot to think about – and some much-needed reassurance.

I bought myself a notebook from the station newsagent's before catching my train. There was so much information racing around in my head I was scared I'd lose it.

So – what did I know? Aiden, Cherie and Dani all worked together at Vaughan-Bayard. After they'd started seeing each other, Aiden had asked Dani to access confidential information – presumably to sell on. Dani had done this, believing at first it was the right thing to do. And then at some point she'd found out Aiden had cheated on her. She'd have felt hurt, angry and, above all, used.

I wondered if Aiden had ever really liked Danielle – perhaps he'd manipulated her right from the start. He'd have broken her heart, I thought, filled with rage and sadness on Danielle's behalf. You had to be seriously cruel to use another person that way.

But there had been more to Dani running away than that. Aiden had mentioned her 'attack of conscience' – and Jed had said Dani had been scared and was thinking of 'speaking up'. And where did the serious side effects come into this?

I laid down my pen and looked out of the window. It wasn't a very interesting journey – right now we were coming into Southampton Airport station. The last time I'd passed through here had been roughly the time Dani had fallen . . .

Why did my mind keep going back to those dowsing crystals? A few had been scattered about the flat when Reece and I had been there. I could remember Dani taking the mick out of them.

Dowsing crystals . . .

I wondered how Cherie had felt when Aiden and Dani had got together. She must have known Aiden was using her to get information, but it still would have made her sour. Dani wouldn't have known that – she thought Cherie was her friend . . .

And then my mind slipped back to the dowsing crystals

and I realized why they bothered me.

When I'd phoned Cherie about Reece's work experience we'd talked about Dani's hobbies. Cherie had reeled off a list – shopping, watching soaps, cinema . . . and dowsing crystals. That had jarred at the time – it sounded so unlike Dani. And it was such a *specific* interest to mention – Cherie wasn't the kind who made mistakes.

Danielle only had one connection to dowsing crystals I could think of – Fay's flat.

How well had Cherie known Dani? Maybe far less than I'd assumed, given that Cherie probably hadn't liked Dani as much as she'd pretended. That list of hobbies was really vague apart from the crystals. Maybe she'd thrown them in because she'd been struggling to think of things?

But to know about the crystals, Cherie would have to have been in Fay's flat. It was the only explanation. And as Danielle had been tracked down by Aiden the weekend she died, that meant Cherie would only have had one opportunity to go there – the Sunday Dani died.

I didn't remember anything of the journey after that. I sleepwalked off the train, across Waterloo station and down on to the Northern line.

My skin was goose-pimpling all over but I felt strangely calm, perhaps because for the first time my thoughts were making perfect sense.

Cherie must have confronted Danielle in the flat. Perhaps she and Aiden had come down to Bournemouth together that weekend. I knew from what Reece had learned at Vaughan-Bayard that Aiden had been furious with Dani for disappearing – he must have been terrified she'd give the game away. Especially if Dani knew that the drug in development had side-effects issues – she might have told Patrick, and then the deal definitely would have been off. The side effects could even have been the nail in the coffin for Dani's involvement. She might be naive with people, but she knew right from wrong. Selling on a drug formula was one thing, but selling on a dangerous drug formula was definitely a bad idea.

Aiden and Cherie had probably decided that Aiden should approach Dani. It had been proved that he'd left before Dani died, but that wouldn't stop Cherie staying behind – I bet she didn't trust Aiden to persuade Danielle to keep quiet. And hey, maybe she'd intended to go one step further and get rid of any physical evidence – Edith, and Danielle's phone! I knew that her phone hadn't been on her when she died and had never been found. But Cherie wouldn't have been able to do anything about Edith – because *I* had her!

The big question was whether Cherie would have been prepared to commit murder.

It was so extreme that I couldn't bring myself to believe

it. Cherie was definitely ruthless, and had probably been seething with jealousy the whole time Dani was with Aiden – but a killer? Maybe her 'chat' with Dani had turned into a fight. Or perhaps she'd come armed and angry . . . which would fit with Dani being afraid enough to back off the balcony.

And all this meant that Dani *wasn't* mentally ill or deeply unhappy – just involved with some seriously bad people.

'It's sketchy,' I muttered to myself. 'But it makes sense.'

But even if I was right about everything, there was still a big problem – proving it.

The next morning I was in a dilemma. I really wanted to make up with Reece and tell him what I'd worked out, but I swiftly realized that it would just make him even more hurt and angry. He'd been pretty clear that he thought pursuing this investigation was putting his family in danger. It was funny, considering how much I thought about the meaning of family, that I hadn't realized how protective Reece was of his.

No, I'd have to give Reece time to cool off before calling him. I was so sure I was right about Dani, but there was no way of proving it. Cherie hadn't left any evidence, and I couldn't even prove that she had been in Bournemouth that weekend. Unless . . .

★

Seven the next evening found me lurking in Vaughan-Bayard's underground car park. I'd managed to slip under the barrier when a car had driven out. Each time someone came down in the lift I ducked behind the rubbish bins. I wasn't sure if anyone would confront me, but I didn't want to run the risk.

It was eerie waiting down there; it could have been any time, night or day, and I wouldn't know. There had to be about sixty parking spaces; most had been vacated. There had been a steady flow of employees leaving since I'd arrived at five thirty, but none of them had been the person I was waiting for.

Though I was uncomfortable and afraid and rapidly losing my nerve, since Bournemouth I somehow felt I was seeing the world with clarity, as though I'd put on a new pair of glasses. In the pocket of my hoody I was hiding a Dictaphone, finger poised to hit the record button. The Dictaphone belonged to Julie – I knew she had it, because I'd used it for a school project about transcribing conversations.

This is a classic scenario for a good reason, I thought. I'd seen it on television over and over again – amateur sleuths confronting criminals who slipped up and got caught on tape. There was absolutely no reason it shouldn't work, providing I was bold enough.

And then the lift doors pinged and Cherie stepped out.

For a moment I was paralysed by a mixture of fear and violent dislike. But then I came to life, jumping out from behind the bins.

'Cherie!'

She turned around. She looked impeccable, even after what must have been a long day. Perhaps she'd popped out at lunch – she was holding a couple of Monsoon carrier bags. Yet again she was wearing shoes the same red as her hair; she looked slightly unreal, like a Cluedo character or something. For a second I hesitated, my finger fluttering over the Dictaphone. Seeing her here, so cool and composed, made me doubt. Could she *really* have pushed my cousin off that balcony? Surely even she couldn't be so ruthless . . . And then I found I didn't care, because this was my moment, and I might not get the chance again. I pressed downwards and felt the tape whirr.

Cherie was just looking at me. The last thing I wanted was to get near to her, but I knew I had to if I wanted a decent recording.

'I want the truth about my cousin,' I said shakily. 'I know you were there the weekend she died.'

She raised an eyebrow, an unimpressed expression on her face; I wondered if she had looked at Dani that way too. 'How long have you been hanging around here?'

'I know you were there.'

'Go home, Sophie.' And Cherie started walking towards

a black Polo parked a few metres away. I started after her.

'I need to talk! I know you killed her!'

Shit, this wasn't going right. Somehow she'd got me flustered, and I had no idea how to save the situation. Cherie ignored me. She pointed her keys at the car and the doors unlocked with a click, backlights flashing in welcome. Cherie opened the boot and began lifting the carrier bags in – and then things unfolded very quickly.

A car shot out of a parking space at the other end of the car park. Its wheels screeched as it zoomed towards us. Cherie glanced up. The car swerved towards Cherie. She started to move, and then there was a scream and a sickening thud and a flutter of red. I flung up my arms to shield myself, unsure what was happening for a few seconds, until I realized that the car was speeding towards the exit and there was a crumpled body lying on the ground.

I stared, transfixed. Cherie was lying on her front and she wasn't moving. I could see what looked like a pool of blood. Her legs were twisted at an unnatural angle; they had to be broken. And as for the rest of her . . .

There was a bleep behind me. A second later someone said, 'Oh my God!' A man and a woman ran out of the lift and knelt by Cherie, both crying out in horror.

'Phone an ambulance!' the man shouted. The woman dug into her bag and suddenly I found I was moving, running towards the exit, desperate to get away. This wasn't real, it couldn't be. One moment she'd been giving me the brush-off – the next, tumbling over the bonnet . . .

And underneath all the horror, I had the cold, terrible realization that I might have just witnessed a murder.

REECE

I was sprawled on the sofa with Mum, watching *The King's Speech*, when the doorbell shrilled. Mum pressed pause on the DVD, looking annoyed.

'Were you expecting anyone?'

I wasn't. I'd planned an early night. My cricket team had a match tomorrow, down in south London, so I'd need to be up early to get the minibus at 7 a.m. Afraid something was up, I shushed her. We waited. A couple of seconds later the bell rang again, accompanied by banging. I pushed the cushion on my lap aside.

'I'll get it. Stay here till I know who it is.'

'Reece, you're being very mysterious,' Mum said. 'It's probably just one of the neighbours . . .'

I wasn't so sure. I edged out into the hallway. Through the glass in the front door I could see the outline of a person. This is just me being jumpy, I thought. After all, if it is Aiden or Cherie come to do something terrible, would they really ring the doorbell?

I opened the door.

'Sophie?' I just about had time to register it was her before she flung herself at me and started to cry on my shoulder. Perplexed and not quite sure how to react, I patted her on the back. I could feel her whole body shaking. Knowing what Mum would say if she saw us, I pushed

Sophie back out on to the doorstep. This was no mean feat. She was hugging me really tightly, as though afraid to let go. Despite the circumstances, I felt a little thrill. Sophie never usually got this close to me.

'Back soon!' I called, shutting the door. I'd be in for an earful later, but I didn't see what choice I had, since Mum had banned Sophie from the house. There was a little green patch further down the road, with a postbox and a bench. I guided Sophie along and we sat down.

Sophie wiped her eyes with the end of her sleeve. She looked half dead. Forgetting how upset I was with her, I put my arm around her.

'What happened?'

After a few moments she croaked, 'A car just mowed Cherie down. I saw everything.'

My jaw dropped. I felt like something heavy had slammed into me. 'Is she dead?'

'Don't know, I didn't go near . . .' She looked at me, and I saw helplessness and horror in her eyes. 'It was so sudden. I just . . . froze. And then I ran. I couldn't bear to look at her . . . Reece, it was awful.'

Somehow I didn't think I was going to be watching the end of *The King's Speech* tonight. Sophie told me the whole story, including everything she'd worked out on her trip to Bournemouth. I listened with a sense of foreboding.

'Christ,' I said when she was done. 'We really are in too deep.'

'It wasn't an accident,' Sophie said in a wobbly voice. 'Someone did that deliberately.'

Cherie . . . may be dead. I couldn't believe it. She had such an indestructible air about her.

Then something more immediate came to me. 'Did they see you?'

'The people in the car?' Sophie stared at me, what little colour there was in her face fading. 'I don't know. It had blacked-out windows.'

'You're in the shit if they did! Listen –' I squeezed her hand. 'We've got to go to the police, Soph. You're a witness to a possible murder now! You need protection!'

I could sense her reluctance even before I finished the sentence. Infuriated, I said, 'This isn't a game! And it's not just about Danielle now!'

Sophie covered her face with her hands. Deciding to give her a minute, I took my phone out of my pocket. I went online and eventually managed to get to the local paper's newsfeed. I wasn't really expecting there to be anything so soon, but I was in for a surprise.

'Sophie! Listen!' I said. 'She's not dead.'

Sophie stared at me. 'What?'

'She's in intensive care – no other details.' I showed her my phone, not sure why I felt quite so relieved. 'You still have to go to the police though. You have to tell them what you saw.'

'Aiden,' Sophie said suddenly.

'What about him?'

'They might be after him too. They might be after everyone who's in on this!'

'We've no way of knowing – we don't even know who the people in the car were. Heck, for all we know it might have been Aiden. Perhaps Cherie isn't his accomplice after all. Perhaps she just found out more than was good for her. Perhaps Aiden never even wanted her involved and she nosed her way in.'

Sophie stared at me. 'Didn't think of that. I was assuming the people in the car were the guys Aiden's been working with – but there's no evidence of that, is there? They could even be on our side, Reece – trying to stop what's going on! We don't know anything.'

She was right. As for Aiden, he was a mystery. And then I remembered – in Aiden's organizer it said he was taking leave tomorrow. He had a meeting with HJP. I wished I knew who HJP was.

But then who said HJP was a person?

'We've been stupid,' I said abruptly. 'HJP's a company, Sophie! Or at least a group of people. They must be the guys Aiden's selling the formula to.' I tapped the initials into Google. None of the results were what I was looking for. But that wasn't a surprise. If these people were going to manufacture someone else's drug illegally, they were hardly going to have a website.

It made total sense now. It was so blatant I was almost impressed. I'd done my research on weight-loss drugs. Though there were things on the market, none really worked. Something that did would make millions. It wouldn't just be bought by people looking to lose a few pounds. There would be big medical implications too. I realized how many diseases were linked to obesity – diabetes, heart disease, even some cancers.

Feeling I'd been quite clever, I explained this to Sophie.

She nodded. 'They must be planning to sell it despite the side effects,' she said. 'How greedy is that? It could do more harm than good. I bet that's why Dani got out! Maybe she even tried to let Patrick know – he could be from HJP. Then the deal would have been blown – hey!' She stopped. 'Did you just say Aiden has a meeting tomorrow?'

'Yup – 7.45 a.m., airport, T3.'

'Someone must be arriving in or leaving London then.'

We stared at each other. I was sure Sophie must be able to hear my brain ticking.

'Aiden must be handing the formula over and getting the money,' I said. It felt totally eerie to be having this conversation out here under the street lights, but also exciting. 'Danielle must have accessed the formula data before she jumped ship. Maybe whoever's picking it up is going straight out to Brazil once the deal's done. Holy smoke, this is it!'

Sophie was shaking her head. 'But this doesn't help at all. We don't know which airport.'

'If we're talking Brazil, I'm fairly certain it's Heathrow – my Aunt Meg went to Rio a few years ago, remember? Mum drove her to the airport. Let's check.' I tapped in Heathrow's web address on my phone. As we were waiting for it to load, I said, 'The big question is, which terminal? Heathrow's got five.'

'You said Aiden's diary said "airport, T3". That could mean Terminal 3.'

'Of course!' But when we got the page up my excitement faded. There were a couple of flights a day to Brazil from Heathrow, but also some from Gatwick. Worse, the Rio and São Paulo flights left from Terminals 1 and 5.

'We don't know for sure that they're going to Brazil,' Sophie said. 'Aiden mentioned Patrick knew people there, but that doesn't mean anything.'

'T3's *gotta* be Terminal 3.' This part had convinced me. 'Maybe whoever Aiden's meeting is flying somewhere else before going to Brazil? Now what, Soph? This is as near to proof as we'll get. D'you want me to come with you to the police now?'

Sophie shrugged.

Instantly I snapped, 'What's it going to take to stop you being so stupid? Someone trying to bump you off too? You have the Dictaphone recording, right? They'll listen!'

'I'm not going through that again!' Sophie shouted. 'The recording doesn't *prove* anything. Anyway, the police don't care about people like me!'

There were so many arguments I could have come back with, but I'd had enough of Sophie's stubbornness. Just how angry I was with her flooded back. She was the most infuriating person I'd ever met. I opened my mouth to tell her so – and then she said in a small voice, 'I'm sorry about last time.'

I wasn't in the mood to forgive her. Too little, too late. Sorry didn't cut it as far as erasing the hurt and anger I was feeling went. 'Whatever,' I said, getting up. 'I'm over it. Forget I ever said anything. It's not like I meant it.'

Sophie flinched. Then she got up and walked away.

Regretting being quite so harsh, I called, 'Please go to the police!'

She didn't reply.

When I got home, I realized I'd gone out without my keys. Mum came to the door with a dark look on her face.

'That was Sophie, I suppose.'

'Don't worry,' I said bitterly. 'I'm *through* with her.'

★

That night I drifted in and out of sleep. Sophie, Danielle, Vaughan-Bayard, the police, everything – it went around and around in my head until I finally decided I might as well get up.

The neon display on my bedside clock showed 5.20 a.m. Aiden would be having that meeting in just over two hours, by which time I'd be on the minibus. By the time I'd showered and put on my cricket whites it was quarter to six. Too restless to kill any more time at home, I decided to grab something to eat and amble schoolwards. After scribbling a note to Mum, I headed out.

The roads were virtually deserted. I tried to focus on the match ahead, but my mind kept slipping back to Sophie. I wondered if she had gone to the police. I knew I should have gone with her.

I was almost at Berkeley when my conscience got the better of me. I took out my phone and dialled her number.

Sophie picked up on the second ring. Alarm bells went off in my head. There was no way in hell she would normally be up this early.

'Reece?' There was a steady chugging in the background. It was hard to make her out. 'I'm about to—'

'This train is for Kennington via Charing Cross,' said

an announcement in the background. Suddenly knowing what all this meant, I yelled, 'Sophie, you—'

And then the call cut out.

SOPHIE

It was 7.25 when the tube pulled in at the station for Heathrow Terminals 1, 2 and 3, all the way out in southwest London. It was busier than I'd expected, but then there were lots of early flights. As I followed people with suitcases up the escalators I heard an announcement saying that the Piccadilly line was experiencing 'severe delays'. I hurried along the travelators to the terminal, coming out into a large modern area with benches, a departure board and lots of people milling around. In front of us was Terminal 3 itself – a long glass-fronted building, yellow signs everywhere.

I had no idea what my plan was. I'd never been less prepared for anything in my life. And I had to admit I was afraid. It felt like I didn't know what I was doing any more. Maybe Reece was right and I was obsessed. When I'd left him last night I really had intended to go to the police. But what could I tell them? If I gave a witness account of what I'd seen in the car park, I would have to explain why I'd been there in the first place, and I didn't care what Reece said – they'd think I was crazy and obsessed, and then Julie would get dragged in, probably my social worker too . . .

But Reece! There'd been so much I'd wanted – planned – to say to him yesterday, but it hadn't worked out.

Stop it, I told myself. I was on my own now and I'd just have to deal with it. Maybe it was easier that way. I took the escalator to the second floor – the downstairs was just the check-in foyer, which presumably Aiden would have no need to use. I realized quickly that the place was nowhere near as big as I'd imagined. The map of Terminal 3 showed that there was only a Costa, a Pret a Manger and one restaurant, and no lounges. Hope surged through me. Aiden couldn't be too hard to hunt down – if he was here . . .

The building was L-shaped. I headed along the wing where Costa was, but it was only small and a glance told me he wasn't there. Beginning to feel anxious, I hurried to Pret. What if I was wrong? He might be at another terminal, or even another airport, or, worse, this might be nothing to do with the formula.

Pret was busy. Families, a big group that looked like a hen party – but there was also a man wearing a mac sitting by himself, a big umbrella propped against the table. He looked a little edgy – and like he was waiting for something. Maybe Aiden was late or had got cold feet . . .

And then I saw Aiden – sitting at a table at the back, a coffee cup and a laptop in front of him. He looked an absolute wreck – unshaven, with dark circles below his eyes. I could tell from his body language that he was tense. Was that because he'd run Cherie down and she'd survived?

Or because he was afraid someone would do the same to him?

Sitting opposite him was a man I'd never seen before, casually dressed, sleeves rolled up. A backpack was on the floor beside him, a travel label hanging off it, and he also had a laptop out. He and Aiden looked like two random travellers simply sharing a table in a busy cafe – which no doubt was what they wanted people to think.

The HJP contact! I thought. I wondered if I could get close enough to see what was going on. Pret wasn't large – there was no real way I could hide, though I was wearing a top with a hood and I had sunglasses. Aiden and the man had chosen a table in a position that made it difficult for me to see their screens. The best bet seemed to be to get behind Aiden – if I craned my neck, I might be able to make out what he was doing.

I entered, taking care to keep out of Aiden's eyeline. Even from this distance I could see that he had a web page open. Praying he wouldn't turn round, I moved closer, trying to look as though I was waiting for someone.

Aiden's browser showed a site I didn't recognize. He wasn't typing or scrolling – the flicker of the screen told me he was pressing refresh, over and over again. Why on earth . . . And then I realized what the site reminded me of. Internet banking. I'd seen Julie do it at home. The logo didn't look like one of the high-street chains.

And then Aiden nodded, and both men closed their laptops and stood up. They shook hands, and I saw Aiden hand over a memory stick. The formula! The man nodded, dropped it in a pocket on his backpack and closed the zip.

Realizing they would have to pass me to get to the exit, I scooted across to a table at the far side. Heart thumping, I sat with my back to the exit, trying to look inconspicuous.

It seemed like an eternity as I waited. When I chanced a glance back, I saw Aiden walking rapidly towards the escalator. The man was heading in the other direction towards the departure gates.

I had to get that memory stick! I followed the man to the check-in area. He joined a queue for a flight to Chicago. Knowing what I was doing was stupid, but unable to prevent myself, I joined the queue right behind him. He didn't react, and I dared to hope he hadn't spotted me back in Pret.

He'd put the USB stick in the backpack's side pocket. I was just inches away from it. As I reached out I felt like a million eyes were boring into me. But just as I was about to reach for the zip, the man shrugged the bag off his shoulders and placed it on the floor. He began feeling about in his jacket pockets, presumably for a passport or ticket. Quickly I knelt down, pretending I'd dropped something. One deft movement and the side pocket was open, the USB in my hand. I stuffed it in my pocket and stood up quickly. I could feel my cheeks burning. Forcing myself not to look back at the man, I pushed my way out of the queue, eyes on the exit.

And then a hand clamped down on my shoulder.

I froze. A familiar voice said, 'That was the handover, right?'

'Reece?' I wheeled around. He was wearing his cricket kit, a half-zipped sports bag slung over one shoulder, his cricket bat sticking out at an angle. He was getting a few funny looks, but I was too relieved to see him to care. He cut me off before I could say anything.

'Don't ask why I'm here. I don't even know. Fill me in.'

I looked over Reece's shoulder. The man was picking up his backpack – he hadn't noticed. I grabbed Reece's arm and hurried him outside. In a few words I explained.

'You nicked the memory stick?!' Reece looked flabbergasted.

I nodded, realizing I was trembling. I could hardly believe I'd been so daring – or kept such a cool head. 'Aiden's got his money. We need to get out, fast!'

'One sec,' Reece said. 'What's the guy look like?'

I told him. Reece darted back inside. A moment later he was back, holding his phone.

'Papped a photo of him,' he said. 'Might come in useful. Now let's . . . Sophie, look!'

Reece pointed. It was Aiden, walking rapidly towards the underground station. I didn't think – I set off after him.

Out of the corner of my eye, I saw Reece raise his phone.

REECE

Mr McIntyre had given me his mobile number in case I'd got lost on the way to his barbecue. I dialled it, praying he'd pick up. Just as I was about to give up, he did.

'Mr McIntyre, it's Reece,' I said, not even pausing to say hello. 'Listen, this'll sound crazy, but you need to trust me. Aiden and Cherie and maybe some of your other employees are selling your new weight-loss formula to a company called HJP – I think they operate illegally from Brazil.' McIntyre tried to interrupt, but I carried on talking. 'I'm at Heathrow Terminal 3 now. Aiden's handed a guy a memory stick and it's got to have the formula on it, cos it looks like a crap-load of cash has just gone into Aiden's bank account.'

'Reece?' McIntyre said. 'What on earth are you talking about?'

'It's all true! I'm calling you because you're the only person who might believe me. Listen, sir, we've got the USB. It's OK. But Aiden's on the move and the other guy will be out of the country soon.'

'This is all too much,' McIntyre sounded rattled. 'First Cherie's accident – now this . . .'

Why was he being so slow to understand? I'd say more if I could, but I was scared of letting Sophie and Aiden out of my sight and I was about to head underground into the station.

'That was no accident – she was run over deliberately. Sophie was there and she saw everything. This isn't a joke! Look, I need to go, and I'm going to lose the signal, but I'm asking – no, begging – you to trust me.'

'What shall I do?'

'Tell the police! Pull this man off the flight for questioning, delay it if you can. They'll listen to someone in your position. You're credible. It'll take too long for me to explain.'

I ran out of breath and waited. After a moment McIntyre's voice came over the line, sounding businesslike.

'What does this man look like?'

Thank God I'd got a photo! 'I'll send a pic over now,' I said. I had to hope this meant that McIntyre would do as I said. Sophie and Aiden were vanishing down the steps into the station. Sophie turned and gave me a pleading look.

'Gotta go,' I said. I could say nothing more. I'd just have to hope he would do the right thing. After quickly emailing McIntyre the man's photo I caught up with Sophie. It crossed my mind how this whole thing had blown up in my face. I'd started off helping Sophie because I'd been curious about whether we could be friends again, and now we were trying to uncover a murder and prevent the sale of a dangerous formula.

But there was no time to mull over how insane this

had become – I had to focus. As we headed down into the station we hit a wall of people. The delays on the line evidently hadn't eased up. I guessed there hadn't been a train for a while, though according to the display board one was due in one minute. Pushing between wheelie cases and people with huge rucksacks, we got closer to Aiden. He was standing right at the edge of the platform.

And then he glanced over his shoulder. Sophie and I both ducked, but we weren't quick enough. Surprise and alarm showed on Aiden's face. He started moving down the platform, pushing past people. We followed. The train thundered in. And then things happened very quickly.

A smartly dressed man I'd never seen before stepped out of the crowd into Aiden's path. For a moment I thought he was just getting in position to get on the train first. But then I saw his hands, shoving Aiden forward. Aiden swayed, off balance, and I realized he was going to fall right into the path of the train. But someone grabbed his arm, pulling him back to safety. Sophie!

The man that had pushed Aiden glowered. He took a step towards Sophie. I did the first thing I could think of, which was to grab my cricket bat from my bag and slam it across the man's chest. He fell back. Then suddenly the train doors opened and people were surging into the carriages.

'Get the hell out!' someone was shouting. I realized it

was Aiden. He'd got on to the train. 'Don't you get it? They'll kill you!'

Whatever else he was going to say was blotted out by the closing doors. I hit the side of the train with my bat, futilely hoping the driver would reopen them. But the train began moving – and I saw that the man was still on the platform. I grabbed Sophie's hand.

'Come on!'

We ran towards the escalators. I had no idea what the man would do next, but instinct told me to get away – *pronto*. At the top of the escalator I looked back. My heart pounded as I saw the man behind us, pushing his way up. Part of me was screaming to run. But another part was telling me to act normal. We had to remain *calm*. As we followed the crowd on to the travelators, the man appeared again – moving even more rapidly. We sped up. It felt like we were moving awfully quickly, and I almost stumbled at the change of pace when we stepped off. The man was still on our tail. What was worse, he seemed to be gaining on us.

We had to get to the open reception area. We could lose him there. Or better still, inside the terminal. There were security guards all over the place. He couldn't do anything to us there.

We hurried off the second travelator and up the stairs. Out in the open we made a beeline for the terminal doors, almost running now. I looked over my shoulder, expecting to see the man bearing down on us – but he had stopped. I blinked; was I seeing things? No – he was heading in the opposite direction, suddenly looking casual and relaxed.

'The hell?' I gasped, looking at Sophie, who was trying to catch her breath. I realized I was still holding her hand. Maybe it had become clear that he wasn't going to catch us, or maybe he'd seen that we were just kids. I didn't like this at all.

'Let's get out of here, Soph. The Piccadilly line's probably still screwed. Want to see if we can get a bus?'

I didn't need to add that I'd rather not go back to the underground after what we'd seen happen to Aiden. Right now, all I wanted was home, and the USB safely out of our hands. I could hardly believe that just a few days ago I'd been thinking this whole thing was exciting, a bit of fun. *Fun?!* I felt small and hopelessly out of my depth, like a kid who'd been shoved into a game where they didn't know the rules and didn't want to play any more.

The bus station was right nearby. We hurried over to look at the timetables – and at that moment a car appeared out of nowhere, overtaking one of the arriving buses and screeching to a halt next to us. The driver wound down the window. He was a bearded man in his thirties who I didn't recognize.

'Reece? Sophie? Get in. Mr McIntyre sent me.'

For a moment I was too surprised to react. 'How come . . . ?'

'No time!' the man said. 'We need to make a move.'

The urgency in his voice spurred me into action. I opened the door, pushing Sophie forward. She hesitated, then scrambled across the backseat. I followed. Almost before the door had closed the man put his foot down and we were off, past the bus and down the road.

I leaned forward. 'What's going on? Is someone following us? Did you manage to stop the man getting on the flight?'

'One moment,' the man said. Suddenly unsure, I opened my mouth to ask another question. But then the car jerked to a halt by the pavement. Startled by the suddenness of the stop, I looked up – and then the front passenger door opened and someone got in.

It was the man who'd tried to kill Aiden.

I grabbed the door handle but the driver moved just a second faster. There was a sickening *click* as he pressed the button that locked all the doors.

'Well,' said the newcomer as the car started moving again. 'That wasn't too difficult.'

SOPHIE

The men didn't take us far. We drove along the road by the bus terminal, then turned left by Hatton Cross station. We turned on to a smaller road, and it was there that the car stopped, in the shadow of a warehouse. An industrial estate, I thought. It reminded me of somewhere Julie had driven out to once to get new tyres for her car. Most worryingly, it was deadly quiet.

If they wanted to do something to us, this was probably the kind of place it would go unnoticed . . .

I glanced at Reece. He'd looked dumbfounded when the man who'd chased us had got in. Something had gone very badly wrong. I thought about Aiden. I wasn't sure why I'd saved him from falling in front of that train – it had been instinctive, one of those things you just *do*. Aiden would be on his way home now, and then he'd probably go somewhere he couldn't be found, with a whopping great sum in his bank account. But I bet he'd be freaking out as much as we were – he'd nearly been a goner back there. Who was to say they wouldn't try to kill him again?

The question now was, What were they going to do with us?

It was the man who'd chased us who broke the silence. His accent was easy to identify – American. I guessed he was probably around the same age as Aiden, with longish light brown hair and expensive-looking sunglasses propped on his head. 'Give it to me.'

Reece and I stayed silent.

'Don't pretend you don't know what I'm talking about,' the man said. 'I know you have the memory stick.'

Reece cleared his throat. 'Look, I dunno who you are or what you want, but there are laws against kidnapping. So you can let us go right now.'

He didn't sound very assertive.

'Just hand it over,' the man said. He paused. 'Believe me . . . it is really not in your best interests to piss me off.'

There was something in the way he said it – slowly and deliberately – that told me I'd better do as he said. I took the memory stick out of my pocket and handed it to the man. So much for trying to play the heroine.

'What were you doing at Heathrow?' the man asked.

'We live nearby.' Reece gave him a blank stare. 'We hang out and watch the planes sometimes.'

'In your sports kit?' He nodded at Reece. 'Sure, I've heard of kids amusing themselves in odd ways, but that doesn't gel. Does the name Aiden Anderson mean anything to you? What about Vaughan-Bayard? Cherie Tapper?'

Neither of us said anything.

'This is useless!' the man said suddenly. 'Waste of time!'

He leaned forward, and for the first time I saw beads of sweat on his forehead. Suddenly he didn't seem so cool, and that was a lot more frightening – especially as I'd caught a glimpse of something under his jacket pocket that looked very like a gun. 'Stop playing dumb and tell me how much you know. This is your last chance.'

'You said Mr McIntyre sent you,' Reece broke in, colour flaring on his cheeks. Alarmed he was going to lose his temper, I laid a hand on his arm. 'Is he in on this?'

'Hardly.' The man made a contemptuous noise. 'I overheard you on the phone to him. Seemed like the best way of getting you into the car without a fuss.' He nodded at the driver. 'Move.'

The driver turned the key in the ignition. Over his shoulder he said, 'Put your seat belts on.'

It was such an absurd thing to say under the circumstances that I almost laughed. As if they cared about our safety!

We drove for about half an hour before the driver pulled in at a large, mostly deserted service-station car park. The man in the passenger seat hadn't left anything to chance; he'd made us hand over our mobiles and he'd even taken Reece's cricket bat, though there was hardly room for him to do any damage with it in the car. The only thing that kept me from absolutely panicking was that we were in a built-up area in broad daylight. The driver – I'd picked up that his name was Kyle – turned the radio on; I'd desperately hoped that something of what was going on would have made it on to the news, but the main item was just some scandal about a football player. But why would it have been us? Sure, Reece had alerted McIntyre, but he might not have taken his call seriously. For all we knew, something nasty might have happened to McIntyre by now. And it would be a long time before Julie or Effie would worry. By then we might not even be alive.

The men got out of the car. 'Don't try anything,' the man who'd taken the memory stick said. 'We'll be right outside, and we'll be disposing of this too.' He picked up Reece's cricket bag and got out, slamming the door. I heard a click as the doors locked.

'On any other day I'd hit the roof about that,' Reece said in a small voice. 'But right now I'm more concerned about whether they'll be disposing of *us*.'

'We've got to think. There must be a way to escape.' I could see through the window that the men were standing just a few paces away, presumably discussing what to do next. Kyle had a blank expression on his face – I hadn't got the measure of him yet – but the other guy was waving his hands about, evidently worked up. I wondered who he was. He seemed to be in charge. Even given how close they were, it might have been worth trying to do a runner – but we were locked in, and Kyle had the key. And the other man had a gun . . .

'D'you think they're going to kill us?' Reece's question hung in the air.

I swallowed. 'They tried to kill Cherie.'

It was the same car – it was so obvious now that I wondered how I hadn't noticed the moment it had appeared. But everything had happened so quickly – I hadn't had a chance to think, let alone make connections. What really worried me was that the men had what they wanted – the USB. If they were going to let us go, surely they would have by now . . .

'Oh God!' Reece's voice wobbled. 'What the hell have we got ourselves into?'

'I should have listened to you,' I said in a small voice. 'I should have gone to the police.'

'Fat lot of good saying that now! It's my fault too. I could've thought, "Screw Sophie!" and gone myself.'

I unclicked my seat belt and shuffled along the seat and reached out to Reece. He shifted so he could put his arm around my shoulders, and I leaned against him, pressing my hand to his chest. It flitted through my mind that under any other circumstances this would have felt weird. This was very definitely a cuddle and not a hug. But that didn't seem to matter – anything that made me feel even slightly comforted was a good thing right now, and being close to Reece did that.

Reece gave me a squeeze. 'Maybe Mr McIntyre will be on the case – assuming they were telling the truth and he isn't in on this.'

'On a scale of one to ten, how convinced do you think he was by your story?'

'About a five?' Reece pulled a face. 'You know how I moan about Mum being clingy? Well, right now I'd be quite happy if she was the most paranoid mother under the sun, cos at least that would mean someone would be freaking about where I was!'

I ran my tongue over my lips. My throat felt dry – but somehow I didn't think the men were going to bother with niceties like water. 'We really are on our own.'

'Bloody useless detectives, aren't we? Hey – you're shaking.'

I gave him a mirthless smile. 'So are you.'

'Guys!' Kyle tapped on the window. 'Less of that.'

'Oh, sod off,' Reece muttered, but we drew apart and I slid back to my seat. Reece reached for my hand and I let him take it. I didn't see how they could complain about that. Kyle noticed as he got in, but he didn't say anything, and the other man was too busy looking at his phone. As the engine fired up, I couldn't help feeling that we could have used that time alone better – hatching a plan or something. But the moment was gone now.

★

We drove along the motorway for what seemed like ages. The road signs told me that we were heading west, away from London and everything I knew. After a while we turned off on to an A-road that seemed to be full of roundabouts, and I lost track of where we were. I'd read a book once where the main character had been abducted. She'd pretended the car journey was making her sick and got the kidnappers to pull over and let her out, and then she'd managed to get away. I doubted I could get that to work – these guys didn't seem that gullible, and it wasn't like there was anywhere to run to. The only good news was that they'd given us something to drink.

Eventually Kyle took us on to quieter roads and through a succession of villages. It was between two of these, in a particularly desolate area of countryside, that we stopped. Our destination seemed to be a little cottage painted a washed-out shade of pink, set away from the road down a bumpy track. I could tell from the state of the garden that it hadn't been lived in recently. The word to describe this place was 'desolate'.

The men bundled us out of the car. The one in charge kicked over a flower pot by the door. Underneath was a key. He opened the door to reveal a bare porch, empty coat hooks either side. Once we were inside he locked the door.

'Keep an eye on them,' he told Kyle, and disappeared through into a lounge area. I heard footsteps as he moved around, presumably checking the place out. I glanced through the door into the sitting room. There wasn't a lot of furniture, just a couple of sofas that looked about twenty years old, an old-fashioned-looking television and some prints on the wall. Everything was coated with dust. There was no way this was someone's house – perhaps it was a holiday cottage of some sort.

After about five minutes the man returned. 'I've secured the pantry. Best room to stow these two. Nice heavy lock.'

'What a wonderful selling point,' Reece muttered. 'Is that what the estate agents tell all the visitors?'

The man stared at him, clearly deciding whether or not that merited a reply. He probably thought Reece was just being mouthy. I knew better – this dark kind of humour was Reece's way of facing reality when things got bad. He'd been like this when his dad died. In the end the guy just told him to shut it. We were marched through into the lounge and then along to the kitchen. There was a heavy wooden door leading to what looked like a large cupboard, shelves stacked with cans.

'Help yourselves to the food,' Kyle said. 'We'll bring some water. Wouldn't want you dying of thirst.'

'Hilarious,' Reece murmured. He rubbed his arms. 'Christ, it's cold in here.'

'I'll see if I can find some blankets,' Kyle said.

'It's not a freaking hotel,' I heard the other man say

as the door closed on us. 'Quit being nice. What the hell are we going to do with them?'

'Your decision, Patrick.' The rest of Kyle's reply was lost as they moved away. Patrick? Unless it was a big coincidence, we'd finally met Patrick from the email messages: Aiden's former friend, who didn't trust Aiden and Cherie – and had nasty associates . . .

I went to the door and rattled the handle, without much optimism. Patrick had been right when he'd said it was a heavy lock.

'No getting out of this one,' I said, watching Reece as he moved around pressing his hands against the stones. I couldn't see him very well through the gloom; I'd tried the light switch by the door, but the bulb hanging above us had blown some time ago.

We sat down together and leaned against the wall facing the door.

'So . . .' Reece said. The word hung in the air for some seconds, hopeless, empty, summing up the situation we found ourselves in.

'So nothing. We're well and truly stuffed.'

The only thing in our favour – ironically – was that we didn't have much evidence against them beyond Dani's iPhone backup. That might make them decide to let us go. If they were going to kill us, surely they would have by now?

'Soph?' Reece asked. I realized I must have been silent a while. I shifted into a more comfortable position, drawing my knees up to my chest, already feeling the chill. For a moment I considered asking Reece if I could huddle up to him – and maybe not just for the heat – but instead I heard myself say, 'I was just weighing up what they're likely to do.'

He let out a hollow laugh. 'Obvious, isn't it? Look at what they tried to do to Aiden and Cherie. They've got the formula. Now they're disposing of the evidence.'

After about half an hour we heard the click of the bolts on the door being pushed back, followed by the key turning. Kyle appeared with a couple of musty-smelling blankets and a big bottle of water. He tossed them on to the floor.

'Either of you need to take a bathroom trip?'

Both of us nodded. Kyle took me out first.

'Who owns this place?' I asked as I climbed a narrow staircase. Kyle had positioned himself behind me so I couldn't do a runner.

Kyle made a non-committal noise. 'That's the bathroom straight ahead. Don't try anything clever.'

I glanced around the landing before going inside. It looked like there were only two other rooms, so the place couldn't be very big. The bathroom was fairly clean, considering how dusty the rest of the house was. The window was tiny, but it was big enough to show that we were in the middle of nowhere. There was a road in the distance, probably further away than it looked. There were certainly no houses I could see and no sounds of life.

Kyle rapped on the door. Quickly I opened the bathroom cupboard, but there was just a toothbrush and a packet of aspirin – nothing that could be of any use.

As Kyle took me back downstairs, I said, 'Our parents will notice we're gone soon. They'll call the police.'

Kyle said nothing, and I found myself back in the pantry as he took Reece upstairs. I shivered and settled down, pulling one of the blankets over me and trying to ignore the smell.

REECE

At about six o'clock I found a can opener and opened a tin of peach slices. I offered them to Sophie.

She shook her head. 'Do you ever think of anything other than your stomach?'

'I've not eaten since six this morning, and I can't see how starving myself is in any way productive.' I fished out a slice from the syrup and slid it into my mouth. It tasted of nothing and I swallowed quickly.

Although my earlier panic had dulled, I was still very, very afraid. I'd desperately tried to come up with escape ideas, but none of them seemed like they'd work. I thought about Neve and Mum. Neve would be at the kitchen table right now with her crayons. Mum would be preparing dinner, grumbling about me not letting her know if I was joining them. It was likely that she'd tried to ring my phone, but my not picking up wouldn't cause much alarm. She'd assume I was playing cricket. My teammates would call when I didn't turn up for the minibus, but again, that would be my mobile number, not home – and as we always took a reserve player, they probably wouldn't be too bothered.

Christ, if I didn't get out of this, what would that mean for Mum? She'd already lost Dad. I didn't want to imagine what losing me might do to her. And would Neve even remember me as she got older? The thought that I might be forgotten was really terrifying. I felt horribly guilty. I'd chosen Sophie over my family. Now I was facing the consequences.

'Sorry I got you into this.'

I glanced sideways. Sophie was slumped beside me, bundled in blankets up to her chin. I waved my hand in front of her.

'OK?'

'No. If it wasn't for me, you wouldn't be here. Your mum was right when she said I was bad for you.'

I shrugged. I didn't have it in me to be angry with her any more.

'Why did you come to Heathrow?' Sophie asked. She had a cobweb in her hair. I reached across to brush it off. 'You didn't have to.'

'Because I wanted to prevent the sale of a dangerous formula, perhaps?' That was only half the truth. I came because despite what I've said, and despite how you infuriate me, I still care about you, I thought. But I didn't say so. She knew, anyway.

'Sophie,' I said, laying my hand on her arm. It wasn't really the right moment, but it might be the only chance I was going to get. 'I know what happened at Paloma's party.'

When she didn't respond I said, 'Paloma told me. We

had a gossip in Waitrose the other day – in the chutney aisle.' If Sophie raised a smile at that, it was there and gone in an instant. 'Why didn't you tell me? I had no idea!'

'Why weren't you there? School was hell for me afterwards – everyone calling me a psycho for going after Zoe like that. Completely getting the wrong idea – I can't even begin to describe it. And I look awful in that video, but I was trying to surprise you by showing I'd made an effort. I was really banking on you being there, Reece . . .'

Sophie had a helpless expression in her eyes. That told me exactly how deep this had gone. I bit my lip, trying not to get too hopeful about Sophie admitting she'd made an effort for me.

'You were acting funny after the play. Then you ignored my texts. I thought you weren't bothered about me any more.'

'Of course I was bothered! That was why I never tried with your new mates – it felt like they were taking you away from me.'

'You thought I'd let that happen?'

'I'm not the easiest friend to have.' Sophie looked away. 'I know that, but seeing you having fun with other people made me think I was in the way. And I saw photos of you at the bar that night enjoying yourself.'

There was a creak from outside. We both tensed, but when nothing happened we relaxed.

'Soph,' I said, 'I'm sorry I let you down. But you get why I didn't come to the party, right?' She nodded. 'Everyone disappoints you once in a while. That doesn't mean you can't trust them any more.'

Sophie's voice was almost inaudible. 'I've been let down so many times, Reece. It's so hard to trust anyone now. It's easier to run away.'

'At risk of sounding like a shrink . . . if you run away from everything, one day you'll look round and there'll be nothing left. Some things are worth sticking with, even if they aren't perfect.' I paused. 'Hey, go me! That was pretty profound.'

She made a snorting sound; for a moment I wasn't sure whether it was laughter or crying. 'Are you saying you're worth sticking with?' she asked.

'Right now you've not got much choice.'

Sophie paused. I got the impression she was weighing up whether to say something or not. 'Those girls . . . You know, the posh ones that joined your mates sometimes. Was there ever anything going on with that blonde one? She liked you. I could tell.'

I wasn't sure what she meant at first. Then I realized. 'Were you *jealous*?'

It was ridiculous, but I couldn't help being pleased. Perhaps she'd been lying when she said she didn't fancy me.

'Maybe.'

'Nothing happened,' I said. 'Know why?' I paused. 'She wasn't anywhere near as interesting as you.'

It was hard to tell, but I was pretty sure she blushed. Crazy hope surged inside me. But all she said was, 'Can we agree that that's in the past? Just . . . it seems unimportant now. I should have talked to you about the party . . . Sorry.'

I was too distracted to reply properly. Her face was really, really close to mine, so close that her hair was actually brushing my cheek. We'd been sitting next to each other so long that I could feel the heat from her body. It was totally the wrong moment, but I was so tempted to lean a few inches closer and kiss her . . . But then voices came from outside. Patrick and Kyle.

SOPHIE

I wasn't sure exactly where Patrick and Kyle were at first. After a moment I realized they had to be on the other side of the wall, outside the house. Hearing my name, I froze, shushing Reece when he opened his mouth.

'. . . said she had a young cousin,' Patrick was saying. 'Knew that girl reminded me of someone. Wonder if Danielle told her anything?'

'No way of knowing for certain.' Kyle spoke more softly; it was hard to make out every word. 'She'll deny everything.'

'Whatever. It's not like Danielle was important. Aiden and Cherie shouldn't have got her involved if she couldn't be trusted. Odd though. She sent me an email saying she needed to talk to me, the day before she died . . .'

Kyle murmured something I didn't catch. Patrick continued, 'Funny how it was Cherie's idea to involve Danielle, considering how it backfired on her. Aiden wasn't meant to end up actually *liking* Danielle.'

I sat up sharply. Kyle said, 'And then she died. Funny, that.'

'Hey!' Patrick sounded annoyed. 'I don't know what happened and I don't much care. She did her bit.'

Hearing them talking about Dani like this stung. But at least it confirmed what I already suspected – Cherie had to be responsible. I might never know the details but at least I had someone to blame. And Danielle *had* tried to contact Patrick to tell him that the drug had harmful side effects. It meant a lot to me to have that confirmed.

'Did you ring São Paulo?' Kyle was asking.

'I'm waiting for a call back. Need advice on what to do with those kids.'

'You've not got too many options, the way I see it.'

'What's all this "you" stuff? You're in this too, Kyle.'

'It's gone too far. Out of control.'

There was a pause, then Patrick said, 'If you're talking about Cherie, she shouldn't have asked for more money. As for Aiden, he's lucky he got away – I'm not convinced he's covered his tracks properly at V-B. If he's found out, he's not going to stay quiet.'

'So what about the two inside?' Kyle asked. 'They're *kids*, for God's sake. They probably didn't realize what they were getting into.'

'They know too much. You see the choice I have here? At the end of the day you can give me this bleeding-heart trash, but I've gotta protect myself. It's too late to backtrack – and we've got the formula, for God's sake. We're almost there. We're going to make millions!'

Kyle's response was inaudible; it sounded like the men had moved away. I let out my breath, realizing I'd been holding it. I could feel that I'd started to shake again – was it only a few minutes ago Reece and I had been talking about Paloma's party, almost as though everything was normal? I wondered when they would make a decision about what to do with us – surely it had to be soon . . .

At 11 p.m. Kyle reappeared with another bottle of water, some cushions and a lantern. He asked if we needed another bathroom trip. When we were both back in the pantry, he told us to sleep.

'Sleep?' Reece sounded incredulous. 'You're kidding.'

Patrick appeared in the doorway, unsmiling. 'Do as he says.'

'Why? You're holding us here against our will.' Reece took a step forward. 'It might surprise you, but I'm not feeling very cooperative! I want you to tell me what you're going to do with us.' He paused. 'Right now.'

He sounded way more assertive than I knew he felt. Impressed but afraid for him, I opened my mouth, but Patrick spoke first.

'No.'

'Why not?' Reece demanded. 'Haven't decided? Or d'you just enjoy being cruel? If it's the first, then that's just pathetic—'

Patrick's hand shot out. I flinched even before I heard the smacking noise; when I looked up again Reece was staggering back, blood trickling from his nose. I rushed over and put my arm around him. 'Is any drug worth killing us for?' I cried. 'It's not even the real deal! Did Aiden tell you about the side effects? It failed the trial! It's gone back for redevelopment.'

Kyle and Patrick froze. Then Patrick grabbed my collar, pulling me forward.

'What?' he demanded. 'You mean to say they've given us a phoney formula? They've double-crossed us?'

Taken aback by the impact my words had had, I stared into his eyes. 'I don't know the details, but I know it's not ready. You're not going to be able to sell it as it is.'

Unless you don't care about the side effects, I thought. If Cherie and Aiden had been ruthless enough to sell a bad formula, then maybe Patrick and his associates would produce the drug anyway. The thought of people taking the drug, full of hope and unaware of what it might do to them, made me feel sick.

Patrick made a growling noise and let go of me. Kyle followed him out, and I heard what sounded like the beginnings of an argument as the door slammed shut.

I looked at Reece. He was mopping up his nose with the end of his sleeve. 'You all right?'

'Yeah. It's not broken or anything. Crikey. What a psycho! You really got to him!'

Whether mentioning the failed trial had been a smart

move or not was something we'd have to wait to find out. I wished I knew what the side effects were, so I could've been more specific.

Not knowing what else to do, we arranged the blankets and cushions into a makeshift bed. It felt like we were just waiting to be killed. What had just happened showed that Patrick had no reservations about hurting us and I wasn't confident Kyle would stop him if he decided he wanted us dead. If the worst was going to happen, I almost wished they'd just get on with it. I couldn't take not knowing much longer.

I shifted on to my side, facing Reece, trying to ignore the edge of one of the stones on the floor sticking into my arm through the blanket.

'Why are they being so indecisive?' I whispered.

'Because we're sweet and innocent and they don't want to have to kill us?' Reece's nose had stopped bleeding by now, but he looked pale. Up close, I could see that his brown eyes had flecks of green in them. How had I never noticed that before? 'Something's gotta shift. Even if McIntyre hasn't called the police, Mum will soon enough.'

I closed my eyes, thinking of all the things in my life that I hadn't done and probably now never would. Sixteen – it was far too young to die.

★

Despite everything, I must have fallen asleep. The next thing I knew I was opening my eyes, feeling like my body was bruised all over. Reece was sitting up, eating from a can with his fingers. I groaned and rolled over.

'What time is it?'

'About half four. Can't sleep. Whatever this is, it tastes mega-gross.'

He got to his feet and began shuffling through the cans on the shelves. After half a minute of listening to the clanking of tins, I groaned. 'How can you think of eating at a time like this?'

'Easily! How can you think of *sleeping*? I'm going mad.' Reece rattled at one of the shelves. It didn't shift. He swore and threw the can on the ground. It bounced and rolled uselessly. Reece stepped over it and stood surveying the door. 'Think there's any chance of us breaking this down?'

I sat up and pushed my hair back from my face. 'There are locks top, middle and bottom. Looks pretty sturdy.'

'Nothing ventured, nothing gained.' Reece squared his shoulders, stepping back as far as he could.

'Hang on, they'll hear—' As I was getting to my feet Reece flung himself against the door. It flew open and with a startled cry he disappeared. I rushed over. Reece was picking himself up from the kitchen floor, rubbing at his elbow. I helped him find his feet.

'What the hell?' I cried.

'It wasn't locked!' Reece said. We both looked back at the room we'd been in for the last twelve hours, unable to believe our eyes.

Reece came back to reality first. 'Run,' he hissed. As I fumbled with the front door, Reece started opening drawers. The scraping of metal sounded very loud in the still of the night. Terrified that Kyle or Patrick would appear any moment I opened the door – it too had not been locked.

'Reece! Come on. What are you doing?'

'Seeing if there are any knives worth taking. I'd feel a lot safer if I had some kind of weapon. But there's nothing.'

Outside I looked around, trying to get my bearings. The cold air tasted delicious after the stale pantry. It crossed my mind that the lantern might be useful, but that would mean going back inside. I heard a sharp intake of breath from Reece. I followed his gaze to where the car was – or rather, where the car had been.

'They've upped and left! Was *that* the plan?'

A light came on in one of the windows on the upper floor of the cottage. There was no time to think and we took off down the dirt track that led to the road. As we ran I heard a smash and an angry shout – from whom, I couldn't tell. At the end of the track we hesitated for a second, then turned right and carried on running.

Several times I stumbled. Were we being followed? I glanced back, but it was still too dark to tell.

'Soph!' Reece was several metres ahead, waiting so I could catch up; he was a faster runner. 'Up here!'

It was a footpath leading into a wooded area, hedgerow on one side. Realizing that Reece's intention was to find a hiding place, I jumped over the ditch and followed, ducking to avoid overhanging branches. Heading into the darkness I thought I heard someone yelling, but if there were any words, they were lost to the breeze.

We crashed through the wood, twigs snapping under our feet. After a few minutes I couldn't take any more and slowed. I took cover behind a pile of logs, bending double and gasping for breath. Reece joined me, craning his neck to see over the top.

'Don't think we're being followed,' he said. 'You OK?'

I nodded. When I'd got enough breath back to speak, I said, 'Let's wait here a moment. It's less exposed than the road.'

Reece sat down on the log pile, wiping his hands on his trousers. 'How long was that door unlocked, d'you think? Come to that, did you even notice Kyle locking it when he went?'

I couldn't remember – but surely we'd have noticed if he or Patrick had come and unlocked it. Maybe Kyle had wanted us to escape. Why? Then I remembered the conversation we'd overheard and everything began to make sense – Kyle had sounded deeply unhappy about what might happen to us. At some point he must have decided the best thing would be to take the car and get out – and while he hadn't freed us directly, he'd given us the biggest chance he could. Wherever you are now, Kyle, I thought, thank you.

Patrick was probably still at large though – and he was the one with the gun. For thirty horrible minutes we stayed put, ready to bolt if there was even a hint that he was nearby. But apart from the occasional hooting of owls, the wood was quiet.

'Let's scoot,' Reece whispered. 'It's going to start to get light very soon.'

Moving as silently as we could, we crept on through the wood. At one point something swooped close to our heads and we both yelped and then ducked, sure the noise must have given us away. But there was silence. After that we moved more freely, though neither of us let our guard down.

The wood was a lot bigger than we had first thought. I started to worry that we were walking in circles, or heading back the way we had come. But then the faint hum of traffic reached our ears and, sure enough, ten minutes later we were on a minor road. The traffic was coming from our left – a little way up we found a junction leading on to a larger road. And there were cars travelling along it. We were back in the real world!

We chose the direction we thought led away from the cottage and walked facing the oncoming traffic, hailing each car that approached. We'd always been warned against hitching lifts, but today it was a risk we were prepared to take. It certainly beat being stuck in a pantry scared out of our wits.

After ten minutes had passed without a single vehicle even slowing though, my optimism faded. Perhaps we weren't going to get lucky – anyone driving along this early in the morning might not think picking up passengers was safe – especially ones that looked like us. Reece's cricket whites weren't white any longer, his trousers splashed with liquid from at least one of cans, and I could see dust and twigs in his hair. I probably looked just as bad.

'So much for human kindness!' Reece shouted as another car zipped past. 'We're going to have to walk to the next town at this rate, wherever that might be.'

'I'm really not liking this,' I said. 'What if—'

'Look!' A truck was pulling into a lay-by just ahead of us. We ran towards it, shouting and waving our arms. The driver stuck his head out of his window.

'Where're you heading?' he shouted.

'Anywhere!' I said. Reece and I clambered inside before he could reconsider. The driver looked at us with a puzzled expression. He was a thickset scary-looking guy with a shaven head, but right now I could've hugged him – in fact I might have done if it wasn't for the Staffordshire bull terrier sitting next to him. It leaned forward and sniffed us with great interest.

'Blimey,' the driver said. 'What you been doing – running away from home?'

'You don't wanna know,' Reece said expressively. 'D'you have a phone we can use? We need to speak to the police.'

'I think you should tell me what's going on first. I don't like the sound of police.'

Reece and I filled him in, just saying we'd been kidnapped and keeping it as brief as possible. When we were done, the driver shook his head.

'Bloody hell! Here.' Reece nearly snatched his mobile out of his hand. 'Don't know whether to believe all this, but you clearly need some kind of help.'

Things happened very quickly after that. The trucker took us to the nearest service station to wait for the police – it turned out we were near Oxford. I didn't really believe they were coming until I heard the siren wailing. It was only in the back of the police car with Reece, speeding towards London, that I at last allowed myself to accept that we were safe.

By the time we arrived at Hendon it was early morning – on a school day I'd be in my first lesson. It felt surreal to be driving through the streets seeing people start their day when I'd been up all night.

Julie and Reece's mum were waiting in the police station. Effie let out a gasp when she saw Reece and flung her arms around him, almost crushing him in a tight hug. I felt a pang of jealousy. Slowly, not meeting her eyes, I went up to Julie.

'Hi,' I said. 'Sorry about this.'

It was such a vapid thing to say, but it was what I felt. Julie had looked after a lot of foster-kids, all with various issues, but she'd probably never had a headcase like me. This escapade would be reported to my social worker, and it was quite possible I'd be moved if Julie felt she couldn't cope. So I was surprised when Julie hugged me. Hesitantly I hugged her back.

'Sophie,' she said softly, 'why on earth did you keep all this to yourself?'

'Because it was the easiest thing to do.' I felt a bit choked up. While there was reproach in Julie's voice, more than anything else she sounded relieved. 'Thought you'd think I was making trouble. I didn't want to get booted out.'

'I'm not going to boot you out, you silly girl.' Julie pushed me back to look me in the eyes. 'Compared to what I've seen before, the "trouble" you're referring to is nothing. Watch my lips: what happens when you turn eighteen is in your hands, but until then, you have a home with me.'

I felt my lower lip quiver. I'd stood on my own feet for so long that this shouldn't matter so much to me . . . but it did. Maybe I shouldn't have closed myself off to Julie. Maybe I shouldn't have made so many assumptions. Maybe people cared more than I realized.

'Thank you,' I whispered.

I looked at Reece. Effie was brushing him down like a dog, getting rid of the cobwebs and surface dirt. It was ridiculous under the circumstances, and he gave me a thumbs-up. I rolled my eyes at him, but I knew I was smiling too.

Lots happened after that. Even though we hadn't slept properly for over twenty-four hours, the police wanted to speak to us. I didn't mind – I wasn't at all sleepy. I guessed I was still on an adrenalin high.

To my surprise, the police officer was DI Perry. He didn't refer to how I'd been dismissed before, and I didn't either. I filled him in – but it turned out he knew quite a bit already. When he told me who his source was, my jaw dropped.

'*Aiden*'s been here?'

Apparently Aiden had called the police yesterday in a panic. DI Perry said he'd been terrified for his life and had told them all about stealing the formula, who he'd sold it to and also about us – though by then the police were already on the case after being alerted by Mr McIntyre. Reece and I had worked out most of this already, though there were a few things we didn't know. Patrick and Aiden had first known each other at university, and Patrick had been at Vaughan–Bayard before returning to the States. Apparently he'd worked for a US pharmaceutical company for a while, before becoming involved with illegal drug production and distribution in Brazil. This was where HJP – a code name for the group – came into it. The cottage we'd been held in was owned by his family. He and Aiden had reconnected at a conference about a year ago, which was where the idea of stealing the formula had come up. The longer-term plan had been to produce it in Brazil and sell it into the USA.

It was now looking like Cherie was off the danger list. I didn't know how I felt about that. I told Perry exactly what I'd seen in the car park, and how the car that had run her down had belonged to Patrick and Kyle.

'Talking of them, do you know where they are?' I asked.

'We'll find them,' Perry said. 'That's all we need from you at the moment, Sophie. I'm guessing you'd like some sleep.'

'What about Danielle?' I asked. 'Have I done enough to prove she was killed?'

Perry met my gaze levelly. 'We'll take a look at that iPhone backup, and then we'll see.'

REECE

I was incredibly miffed that the police seemed to know everything already. DI Perry said that the evidence we'd gathered and our testimonies were important, but it was hardly satisfying. Sophie would say the end result was what mattered, but I'd rather wanted my fifteen minutes of fame.

As we drove home Mum kept looking at me as though she couldn't believe I was really there. As soon as we got in, Neve barrelled down the stairs shrieking happily. I lifted her into a big hug.

'Where were you?' she asked.

'Battling gangsters, armed only with a cricket bat,' I said. 'I reckon I deserve a Wikipedia page for that. Bit scary, but I'm fine.'

'Did you miss me?'

'Duh,' I said, giving her a kiss.

'They weren't gangsters,' Mum said. 'If you're going to brag, at least get your facts straight.'

The logical thing to do was go to bed. I could feel my eyelids dropping. But I wanted to speak to Mum first. She asked Aunt Meg (who'd been babysitting ever since Mum had reported me missing) to take Neve out so we could have some privacy.

We sat in the front room on the couch. I could see

the DVD of *The King's Speech* on top of the television. It seemed ages ago that we'd been sitting here watching it. I'd have to catch up on it sometime.

I cleared my throat. 'I know you're pleased to see me and all, but—'

'Pleased?' Mum interrupted. '*Pleased* doesn't begin to cover it! I thought I'd never see you again, that you might be dead . . .' She wiped at her eyes. I winced. I hated seeing my mother cry.

'Guess you're mad at me.'

'I'm mad at you for not telling anyone what you were doing! That was stupid, and dangerous, and you and Sophie are lucky to be alive. And as I understand it, the burglary and Neve going missing at Brent Cross happened because of this too. So yes, I'm not going to lie, I'm pretty mad. But as well as that −' she squeezed my hand − 'I'm really *proud* of you, Reece. And I know your dad would be too.'

I wished she hadn't brought Dad into it. The last thing I wanted was to feel teary. 'I was trying to protect you and Neve, y'know. Because I love you both, and if anything ever happened . . .'

'Oh, God,' Mum sniffed. 'You're setting me off again. I think we're both too tired to be having this conversation.'

There was one question I still needed to ask, and I had the strangest feeling Mum knew it was coming.

'D'you blame Sophie for this?'

'She's very important to you, isn't she?'

Crap, she knew. But then even Neve had some idea how I felt about Sophie. I guessed it must be obvious to everyone except Soph.

'She's my best friend,' I said carefully. 'I know you hate her, but it was out of order to ban her from the house. Brent Cross was my fault, not hers.'

Mum pursed her lips. 'You make sure that girl appreciates what an amazing friend you are to her. Right now, I don't think she does.'

'You haven't answered the question.'

She sighed. 'I can't stop you from doing the things you want to and seeing the people you want to, can I? You're not my little boy any more.'

I could see it was all I was going to get. I stood up. In the door to the hallway I paused. 'Hey . . . Mum? Did my team win the match yesterday? I mean, I totally would have been there, but I was a bit preoccupied.'

'What? I don't know, Reece! You and your cricket!'

'I'm going to need a new bat,' I said, going upstairs. Mentioning cricket had reminded me of those tickets McIntyre had given me. There were two of them. The match wasn't for a little while, but I knew who I was going to take. I wasn't just going to ask her as a friend either. The big question was whether or not she'd accept . . .

SOPHIE

'Wasn't meant to fricking rain,' Reece said, for the hundredth time. 'This has been one of the driest summers on record. So why, I want to know, is this afternoon the exception?'

'You're not going to get answers by staring aggressively at that can of Coke,' I said. I glanced out of the window of the pizza place we were in. Rain droplets were running down the glass, and the pavements were shiny. 'Lighten up! We only lost an hour's play. I'd quite happily trade that for the rain dance we saw.'

We'd just come from the Oval. As it turned out, the tickets McIntyre had given Reece were expensive balcony seats. The expression on his face when he'd seen where we were sitting had almost given me a stitch I was laughing so hard. Most of the day the sun had shone and we'd sat back in our seats taking in everything and exchanging light-hearted jibes with some India supporters sitting nearby. But then after the tea break the heavens opened, just as it looked like England were gaining the upper hand. The India supporters had launched into a very enthusiastic and very funny dance in celebration.

It had certainly given us a lot to talk about over dinner. We'd also had a small argument over who was paying. Reece had offered, I'd said I wanted to pay my half, and then he'd accused me of 'rejecting his attempt at being chivalrous' and made out he was upset. He wasn't really, and I was happy enough to let him pick up the bill. It felt strange and somehow grown-up for him to be paying for me. I guessed I would have to get used to all this if I was going to be his girlfriend.

I'd realized that deep down I really did like him – and if I was honest, I probably had for a while. I'd just been too afraid that it would spoil everything. But Reece's point about me needing to trust people had hit home. After spending most of the summer together, I missed him badly the first week of sixth form. I'd picked up my GCSE results a few days after Heathrow, and to my astonishment I'd done really well, exceeding most of my predicted grades. I'd even got an A★ in geography, something I never would've thought possible. Reece's results had been pretty good too. Zoe Edwards had done surprisingly badly; she'd been allowed into the sixth form, but she was noticeably subdued and more or less left me alone. Paloma's party was old news now anyway.

It was Paloma who made me act on Reece. We were in Broom Hill's library and I'd ended up filling her in on everything that had happened over the summer. Before I even got to the end, she shrilled, 'Sophieeee! Are you going out with him yet or what? Because if you aren't, you are totally missing a trick.'

This was absolutely typical. So much for kidnapping and murder and pharmaceutical espionage – all Paloma was interested in was my love life.

'This is a silent library!' barked the librarian, glowering at us from the check-in desk. Paloma ignored her.

'Seriously, girl,' she whispered, 'how much more does someone have to do for you to agree to go on a date with them? Climb Mount Everest, rescue a baby from a burning house? Get outta the library right this instant and give him a call, else I swear I will do it myself.'

In the end I went round to Reece's house that same evening. I wasn't sure what I was going to say, but he brought it up first. We were in the garden, sitting on the grass and drinking some disgusting but strangely addictive blue drink Reece had found in Londis in Hendon. Effie was inside having coffee with Reece's aunt. She'd relented on her house ban, but I could tell she still didn't like me coming over. 'You know those Oval tickets,' Reece said. He had his shades on so I couldn't see his eyes. 'There are two of them.'

'Congratulations,' I said. 'You can count. I knew there was a reason you got an A in maths.'

'One's obviously for me. I was thinking, you might like to come too?'

'Is this a date?' I asked.

'I was getting to that,' Reece said. 'You ruined my

moment.' I waited for him to continue. 'So . . . how about it? I know you said it wouldn't work, but I figure impossible, magical things can happen when you're trapped in a dark pantry together.'

He said it so lightly that if I didn't know him better I might have been fooled into thinking it didn't matter.

'The pantry magic's worked,' I said, blushing a little. Reece flipped his sunglasses on to his head, blinking.

'What?'

I fiddled with a strand of hair. 'I couldn't have done this without you. You're a bit of a hero. Just took me a while to realize. It's like you said – some things are worth sticking with.'

Reece looked smug. 'I was a brilliant shrink, wasn't I? Maybe a new career beckons.'

'Thought you wanted to go into the pharmaceutical business,' I said, giving him a push.

It was a lot easier than I thought, getting used to Reece as a boyfriend. The first time we kissed, in his room later that evening, felt a little weird. We'd been talking about something to do with school and then, breaking off mid-sentence, Reece suddenly leaned in, pushing my hair away from my face. Our lips met for a few seconds before he pulled back, and I could tell he felt as self-conscious as I did, because he said, 'I sort of planned that as being better.'

'How much better?' I asked, and that made us laugh and

after that it was more relaxed, and the kissing did improve – and I mean a lot. By the time the match came round, it felt absolutely normal and right. And I'd even bought a dress similar to the one he'd pointed out in that shop window on the way to McIntyre's barbecue. Not that I was going to change what I wore completely, but it was nice to have something new that made me actually feel pretty. And he'd been right: it suited me.

'Didn't get to do half the things I wanted to this summer.' Reece's eyes were on the kitchen. Two pizzas that looked like they might be ours were coming. 'I was too busy chasing gangsters. I blame you.'

'They weren't gangsters. How many times do me and your mum have to tell you?'

'If I say it enough you'll believe it.'

The pizzas arrived. I picked up a slice, then paused. 'You know what freaks me out? If I hadn't happened to find that memory stick that day, things would be a lot different right now. We wouldn't be sitting here together, for one thing.'

'It hurts my head if I think about it too much,' Reece said, picking up the biggest slice. 'Eat. That's easier.'

It definitely was. I smiled at him, thinking that it made a change to feel happy, and Reece smiled back. As I took a mouthful, it struck me that it didn't feel like the past was looking over my shoulder any more, bleeding into the present. The past was exactly that – the past. And now I could get on with the future without being afraid.

But I still had one more door I needed to close.

The police were continuing to tie up loose ends. There would be a huge court case somewhere down the line. I was dreading having to testify, especially giving my eyewitness account of Cherie's accident. At least the police had found Patrick – they'd actually picked him up the same day they'd found us, trying to get a flight out of Heathrow. They'd also identified a number of others who'd been involved in the South American drug cartel. Kyle had vanished, but I was happy with that. If it wasn't for him, I might not be here now.

I wasn't sure what would happen to Aiden. He'd probably get a more lenient sentence because of how he'd helped the investigation. I still couldn't believe he'd told the police everything of his own accord – but I guessed any amount of money became irrelevant when you were scared for your life. When push came to shove, it seemed his heart hadn't been one hundred per cent in it after all.

As for Cherie, she'd admitted to going to the flat and seeing Danielle. It had gone more or less as I'd thought. They'd had a row. Cherie had picked up a knife, intending to threaten Dani to keep quiet about the trial results, and Dani had backed away and fallen off the balcony. Cherie was pleading manslaughter. Whether she was telling the full truth or not, I would never know.

By the time I felt emotionally strong enough to go to the cemetery a month had passed. Reece offered to come with me, but I don't think he was at all surprised by my reply that I had to do this alone.

The afternoon was bright and warm and still, the sky an expanse of blue. I walked along the main path slowly, carrying a big bouquet of yellow roses. They had been Dani's favourites.

I found her headstone and stood looking at it. Then I reached down and placed the flowers in front of it.

'I always knew you didn't kill yourself,' I said to her. 'And if the trial goes right, which I really hope it does, everyone else will too. You probably believed you were doing the right thing, making the drug more widely available – and when you realized it was wrong, you tried to stop it.'

It was odd – I'd expected this to make me feel good, triumphant even. But all I felt was relief that it was all over.

I spent a good hour by the grave, remembering Dani. I wondered how many people had really known her; too few, I suspected. Her 'friends' at Vaughan-Bayard had got her killed, and the only man she'd ever loved had been manipulating her. It seemed a sad existence for someone I knew to be warm and generous and clever, and who had deserved so much more.

But thanks to the events of this summer and all the good times we'd shared before that, at least I would remember her – and make sure I never forgot.

ACKNOWLEDGEMENTS

Once again there are a number of people who've helped make *Forget Me Never* happen who deserve big thank-yous. Top of the list are my parents, Sheila and David, who were part of many epic 'Help, I'm blocked on book 2' sessions where we batted around ideas and solved problems. Once again, my agent Becky Bagnell and my editor Emma Young, for all their contributions and professional advice. It goes without saying that thanks are also due to all the lovely people at Macmillan who've helped form the book.

There's also Matt Davison, who knows more about pharmaceutical drug espionage than he perhaps ought to, and Jenny Dixon, who was my partner in crime for the grand research mission to Heathrow. Thank you as well to my brother Luke for writing hilarious notes all over my manuscript (he also said he didn't want a dedication, but is getting it anyway). Given the amount of time me and my netbook have spent there, I definitely need to give a big thumbs up to the staff at my local Caffè Nero and their excellent soy milk latte-making skills.

And last but not least, thanks to everyone – friends, family, colleagues and readers – who has been so very nice about *Pretty Twisted*. Your enthusiasm and support have been a big encouragement to me.

PRETTY TWISTED

GINA BLAXILL

As the train entered the tunnel, it struck me just how bizarre this all was. It could be a chick-flick tag line: 'girl likes boy but keeps it hidden as she helps boy search for the girl he loves'.

Ros met Jono online just a couple of weeks ago. Now Jono's beautiful ex-girlfriend Freya has disappeared without a trace . . . and disturbing evidence is coming to light. So Ros agrees to help him search for her – but she is hiding a secret of her own.

This is only the beginning.

This story is about to get PRETTY TWISTED.

MICE

Gordon Reece

It had to be quiet. It had to be private. We were 'mice' after all. We weren't looking for a home. We were looking for a place to hide.

Sixteen-year-old Shelley has been badly bullied at school. And her mum has been left reeling by her recent divorce from Shelley's overbearing dad. So Shelley is optimistic when they move to a cottage in the middle of the quiet countryside – a place where they can be happy at last.

But then one night someone breaks into their house . . .

In the twisted tale that follows Shelley finds herself wondering – if she and her mum aren't mice after all, what are they?